COLIN DEXTER

The Silent World of Nicholas Quinn

Retold by Anne Collins

BROOKSBY MELTON COLLEGE
OFFICIAL
★

MACMILLAN

INTERMEDIATE LEVEL

Founding Editor: John Milne

The Macmillan Readers provide a choice of enjoyable reading materials for learners of English. The series is published at six levels – Starter, Beginner, Elementary, Pre-intermediate, Intermediate and Upper.

Level control
Information, structure and vocabulary are controlled to suit the students' ability at each level.

The number of words at each level:

Starter	about 300 basic words
Beginner	about 600 basic words
Elementary	about 1100 basic words
Pre-intermediate	about 1400 basic words
Intermediate	about 1600 basic words
Upper	about 2200 basic words

Vocabulary
Some difficult words and phrases in this book are important for understanding the story. Some of these words are explained in the story and some are shown in the pictures. From Pre-intermediate level upwards, words are marked with a number like this: ...³. These words are explained in the Glossary at the end of the book.

Contents

A Note About This Story

At the age of fifteen or sixteen, students at schools in the UK take examinations in all the subjects which they are studying. These are called 'public examinations'. Many students stay at school until they are eighteen. At that age, they take more difficult public examinations. Their grades in these examinations help them to get into universities.

Public examinations in the UK are not set[1] by the schools, or by the government. The examinations are set by groups of experts[2] in each subject from the universities. Several different groups, or syndicates, from different universities, set these exams. The heads of schools can choose which syndicate's examinations their students take.

These syndicates also set examinations for students outside the UK whose first or second foreign language is English. These students write their examination answers in English.

This story is about a syndicate in Oxford – the Foreign Examinations Syndicate – which sets examinations for foreign students. It is not a real syndicate. There has never been a real syndicate called this. A country called Al-jamara is part of this story. This is not a real country.

In the UK, there are many different police forces. Each one works in a large area of the country. The Thames Valley Police is a real police force, and its headquarters is in the northern part of Oxford. But the policemen in this story are not real people, and the things which happen in this story never really happened.

Colin Dexter has written many novels about Chief Inspector Morse and his assistant, Sergeant Lewis.

1

The Foreign Examinations Syndicate

It was a fine summer afternoon in the south of England. A meeting was taking place in a large, comfortable room in Oxford. It was a meeting of the members of the Foreign Examinations Syndicate.

The members of the Foreign Examinations Syndicate were twelve people from different colleges of Oxford University. Each person had an important job in their own college and each of them was an expert in a different subject. Six times every year, they met together to discuss the Syndicate's examination policy – the way that the examination system should work. The meetings were always held at the Syndicate's headquarters, a large old building in a quiet road in the northern part of Oxford.

The members of the Syndicate were called Syndics. All twelve of them were at the meeting that afternoon. And, as usual, a thirteenth person was there too – Dr Tom Bartlett, the Administrator[3] of the Syndicate.

Dr Bartlett was not a Syndic. He was a member of the Syndicate's permanent staff. He had a different kind of job from the other people in the room. *Their* work for the Syndicate was only a small part of their lives. Most of the time, they taught students in the colleges of Oxford University. Bartlett worked for the Syndicate all the time – that was his only job.

There were other permanent members of the Syndicate's staff. They worked for Dr Bartlett and, like him, they had offices in the Syndicate building. But only Dr Bartlett took part in the meetings of the Syndics.

The reason for the meeting, that fine summer afternoon, was to appoint[4] a new member of the permanent staff. This person would work for Dr Bartlett at the Syndicate's headquarters. He or she would be someone who had studied at a university – a graduate. The new member of staff would replace a man called George Bland. Bland had left his job a few months earlier and had gone to work in the Government Education Department of Al-jamara, a small country in the Middle East.

That afternoon, the twelve Syndics and Dr Bartlett had interviewed[5] five people. The interviews had taken three hours, and now the thirteen people in the large, comfortable room had to decide who was going to get the job.

The Dean of the Syndicate – the most important member – turned to the Administrator. 'Dr Bartlett, the person who we choose will work for you,' he said. 'What did *you* think about the people who we interviewed?'

Bartlett was a small, plump man of about fifty-seven. His eyes were bright behind his round spectacles.

'Well, Dean,' he replied, 'I think that two of the interviewees – Quinn and Fielding – were very good. They both

know a lot of things which would help them to do this job well.

'But I must say this – Quinn does have a problem,' Bartlett went on. 'He's very deaf. And in this job, you need to hear well. You have to hear everything that is said in meetings, and you have to use the phone a lot. Perhaps Quinn's deafness would stop him doing the job well. I think that the other man – Fielding – would be the best person for the job.'

Several of the other Syndics were nodding their heads, agreeing with Bartlett. The Dean was nodding his head too. He didn't really care which of the two men got the job. But he wanted the meeting to finish quickly. He was thinking of the work that he still had to do in his own college. And he had another meeting at six o'clock!

'Good,' he said, writing a few notes on a piece of paper. 'Then, if everybody agrees with Dr Bartlett, we'll give the job to Fielding. Now —'

'May I say something, Dean?' said another member of the Syndicate.

The Dean looked up in surprise. The speaker was Christopher Roope, a Chemistry lecturer at Christ Church College. Roope had only been teaching at the university for two years and he was very different from the other Syndics. He was a young man, with long hair and a beard, and he looked more like a student than a teacher.

'Yes, Mr Roope?'

'I'm sorry, Dean,' said Roope, 'but I don't agree with Dr Bartlett about Fielding. I think that Quinn is the best person for the job. He's clever and he's very honest.'

'But he's deaf!' said Bartlett crossly[6]. 'Quinn won't be able to hear what people say in meetings.'

'He doesn't need to *hear* people speaking,' replied Roope. 'Quinn can lip-read very well. When people speak, he watches their lips and he sees the shapes of the words. So he can follow the conversation – he knows what people are saying. He didn't have any problems understanding us during his interview, did he?'

'Well, no,' Bartlett replied, 'that's true. But what about the phone? How can he talk to people on the phone if he can't hear them clearly?'

'Deaf people can get a special kind of microphone,' said Roope. 'They wear it next to one ear, and they can hear a person speaking on the phone quite clearly. I'm sure that Quinn won't have any problems with the phone.'

Bartlett stared at Roope angrily. Why was Roope being so difficult? Why did he want to give the job to Quinn and not to Fielding? Now the other Syndics were looking unsure. At first, they had been certain that Fielding was the best person for the job. But now they were listening to Roope and they were beginning to feel sorry for Quinn.

Roope held up a piece of paper. He spoke to the Dean.

'This is a copy of the Syndicate's rules,' he said. 'May I read one of the rules to you?'

The Dean was looking tired. Now, he wouldn't be able to get back to his college early.

'All right, Mr Roope,' he said. 'But please be quick.'

'This is an important rule,' Roope said. He started to read aloud. 'The Syndicate must employ at least one person with a physical disability[7].' Roope put down the paper and looked at his colleagues[8]. 'Now, Dr Bartlett,' he went on, 'how many people with physical disabilities does the Syndicate employ at the moment?'

'Well – none,' said Bartlett.

'Then we must give the job to Quinn,' said Roope. 'Deafness is a physical disability.'

The other Syndics were thinking. Perhaps Roope was right about Quinn. Quinn was deaf, but he was very clever and honest, and he could lip-read well. He would be able to understand people in meetings easily. He would find a way of understanding people on the phone. Perhaps his deafness wouldn't be a problem.

'Very well,' said the Dean. 'Let's vote on this. If you think that Fielding is the best person for the job, hold up your hand.'

Five Syndics held up their hands.

'And if you think that *Quinn* is the best person, hold up your hand.'

Six of the people round the table held up their hands. The Dean and the Administrator of the Syndicate weren't allowed to vote.

'Good!' said the Dean. 'Then Quinn will have the job. Please write to him tomorrow, Dr Bartlett.'

'Very well, Dean,' replied Bartlett. But he wasn't happy.

'We've made a mistake,' he was thinking. 'A terrible mistake!'

2

Visitors From Al-jamara

Three months later, Nicholas Quinn was working at the Foreign Examinations Syndicate. He often had meetings with the Syndics who were experts in History and English. Together, they set the exam papers in those subjects.

Quinn's office in the Syndicate building was big, bright and very comfortable. It had previously been the office of George Bland, his predecessor – the graduate who had had the job before him.

When Quinn had first started working at the Syndicate, he hadn't been very worried about his deafness. He didn't have a problem when he could see people talking – he could read their lips easily. But talking on the phone *had* been a problem for him, and now he was beginning to worry about this. When people spoke to him on the phone, he couldn't hear their words clearly. He tried hard, but there was room for improvement[9]. He sometimes misunderstood people and this embarrassed[10] him very much. He knew that he'd have to do something about this problem soon.

The phone was a problem, but Quinn enjoyed his new job, and he enjoyed getting to know his colleagues at the Syndicate's headquarters. There were three other graduates on the permanent staff. They worked for Bartlett in the same kind of job as Quinn. They were Philip Ogleby, whose subject was Mathematics, Donald Martin, whose subject was Science, and Monica Height, whose subject was Foreign Languages.

There were many secretaries in the building too, and there was lots of work for them. Question papers for the exams had to be sent to foreign countries. Then, when the students' answer papers were sent to Oxford, these papers had to be sent to examiners in other parts of Britain. These examiners read and graded the answer papers. Most of the secretaries were busy sending and receiving papers, writing to examiners, and keeping records of grades. But Bartlett and the four graduates each had a secretary of their own. These secretaries typed letters for their bosses, and did other work for them. Nicholas Quinn's secretary, Margaret Freeman, had been George Bland's secretary too. But she was very happy with her new boss.

Quinn liked all his colleagues, but he was especially interested in Monica Height. Monica was thirty-four years old and very attractive[11]. She was divorced from her husband, and she had a sixteen-year-old daughter called Sally. One day, Quinn had taken Monica for a drink and a sandwich in a pub[12]. He'd enjoyed the hour that he'd spent with her. He hoped that she would become his special friend.

But there was something that Quinn didn't know. Monica was having an affair[13] with their colleague, Donald Martin. Martin was married, but he no longer loved his wife and he enjoyed making love with Monica. Monica enjoyed it too, but she often worried about her affair with Martin. She was afraid that Dr Bartlett would find out about it, and that he might make trouble for her. Sometimes she told Martin that she wanted to end their affair. But Donald Martin never worried when she said this. After a few days, Monica always wanted to make love with him again.

———

One afternoon in late October, the telephone on Nicholas Quinn's desk rang. Quinn picked it up. Bartlett was calling him.

'Please come to my office immediately, Quinn.'

'I'm sorry, Dr Bartlett,' said Quinn, 'but I can't hear you very well. I'll come to your office immediately.'

'That's exactly what I asked you to do!' said Bartlett. 'What did you say?'

11

In his own office, Bartlett put down the phone angrily.

'It's very difficult to work with Quinn sometimes,' the Administrator thought. 'It's Roope's fault. Why did that stupid man make the Syndics give Quinn the job? He's made a lot of problems for the rest of the permanent staff!'

When Quinn entered the Administrator's office a few moments later, Bartlett said, 'Sit down, Quinn. I want to tell you about a very important meeting.'

'Next week,' Bartlett went on, 'Sheikh Ahmed Dubal of Al-jamara and four of his ministers are coming to visit us in Oxford. They'll be here on the 4th, 5th and 6th of November. They want to discuss a new History exam for the schools in their country.'

'Al-jamara?' asked Quinn. 'Isn't that where George Bland is working now?'

'Yes, that's right,' Bartlett replied. 'Bland is working in the Education Department there. He's in charge of all the country's public examinations.

'Al-jamara is very important for this Syndicate,' the Administrator continued. 'It's been using our exams for five years now. It's a rich country and it pays us well. So we want to keep the Sheikh happy. I don't want anything to go wrong with this visit. Do you understand me?'

'Yes, Dr Bartlett,' replied Quinn. 'I understand you.'

———

During the next few days, Quinn felt very nervous about Sheikh Dubal's visit. He'd heard a lot of things about the Sheikh, and they weren't all good things. The Sheikh was certainly a strong and powerful ruler, but he wasn't very popular in his own country. Many people said that he didn't rule Al-jamara in a good or honest way.

It wasn't that which worried Quinn, though. He was worried that he wouldn't be able to read the Sheikh's lips. What would happen if he didn't understand the ruler and he made a stupid mistake? If that happened, the Syndicate might lose their business with Al-jamara and Dr Bartlett would be very angry. Quinn knew a lot about Bartlett now. The Administrator had worked for many years to make the Syndicate successful and he was very proud of it.

But when the Sheikh and his ministers arrived, Quinn found that he could understand them very well. He had no problems with reading their lips. They spoke English clearly and beautifully and they were very pleasant people. Quinn liked them.

The visitors were in Oxford for three days. Their meetings with the Syndics and the graduates were very successful. Between the meetings, there were excellent lunches and dinners, and lots of interesting conversation.

On the evening of 6th of November, Sheikh Dubal invited all twelve of the Syndics to dinner at his hotel, together with their wives and husbands. Dr Bartlett and the four graduates from the permanent staff were invited too, together with their partners.

During the dinner, the Sheikh sat beside Monica Height and he obviously enjoyed her conversation very much. Monica looked beautiful as she laughed and talked happily with him.

Donald Martin, Monica Height's lover, was sitting oppo-
site Monica and the Sheikh. Martin wasn't looking happy at
all. His wife, a small quiet woman, was sitting beside him.
She wasn't interesting or pretty like Monica, and Martin
didn't speak to her very much. Martin was watching Monica
and the Sheikh, and he was becoming angry and jealous!

After the meal, Nicholas Quinn watched the Sheikh talking to people. He watched the ruler's lips closely and he
could understand what the Sheikh was saying easily. The
Sheikh had private conversations with several different people, when he whispered his words very quietly so that nobody
else could hear. But Quinn could understand what he was
saying very well.

Suddenly, as Quinn watched the Sheikh talking to one of
the guests, he had a shock. Had he read the Sheikh's words
correctly or had he made a mistake?

By midnight, most of the Sheikh's guests had left the hotel.
But some people remained in the room – the Sheikh and his
four ministers, the Dean of the Syndicate, Monica Height,
Philip Ogleby, Nicholas Quinn, Christopher Roope and Dr
Bartlett and his wife.

Quinn was feeling hot, tired and sick. He had eaten and
drunk too much and it was time for him to go home. He had
to get up early the next day.

As he was getting ready to leave, Bartlett and Sheikh
Dubal walked over to him. Suddenly Quinn was a little
afraid. What was Bartlett going to say?

The Administrator smiled at him in a friendly way.

'Did you enjoy yourself this evening, Quinn?' he asked.

'Oh – yes, very much, sir. Thank you both very much for
inviting me,' said Quinn.

'It was a great pleasure to meet you, Mr Quinn,' the
Sheikh said.

Quinn thanked Sheikh Dubal again and walked outside. He stood for a few minutes, enjoying the cold night air. He hadn't noticed that somebody had followed him outside. But suddenly he felt a hand on his shoulder. He turned and saw his colleague, Philip Ogleby.

'I enjoyed this evening,' Ogleby said. 'Didn't you, Quinn?'

Quinn thought for a moment. 'I want to talk to you, Ogleby,' he said. The two men walked away together.

3

Looking for Dr Bartlett

On the afternoon of Friday 21st November, Christopher Roope was in a train, travelling from London to Oxford. He was sitting in a first-class compartment[14], reading a report. It was the report of the previous week's meeting of the Syndicate. Bartlett always sent the reports of meetings to each of the Syndics, so that they could check them for mistakes. Outside, the rain splashed against the windows of the train.

At four o'clock, Roope finished checking the report. He wrote something on the first page, and put the report into a large envelope. Then he wrote Dr Bartlett's name on the front of the envelope. A few minutes later, the train stopped at Oxford station. Roope got out and waited in the queue of people at the ticket barrier[15]. When he reached the barrier, he spoke to the ticket collector.

'I owe you some money,' he said. 'I travelled from London in a first-class compartment, but I only have a second-class ticket.'

The ticket collector looked surprised.

'That's all right, sir,' he said. 'I won't make you pay the extra money. But thank you for being honest.'

There was a queue of taxis waiting outside the station. Roope got into the first one and told the driver to take him to the Syndicate building.

It was 4.25 when the taxi arrived at the Syndicate's head-quarters. Roope gave the driver a very large tip[16] and he went inside the building. He went straight to Dr Bartlett's office. He knocked on the door, and when nobody answered, he opened it. As he opened the door, he thought that he heard a noise inside the room. But Bartlett wasn't in his office. Nobody was there. There was a large note on the desk.

FRIDAY, 1 p.m. I'VE
GONE TO A MEETING
IN BANBURY. I
MIGHT BE BACK AT
ABOUT 5.30 p.m.

Banbury was a small town about twenty miles from Oxford.

Roope saw another, smaller note on the desk too. He was going to enter the room when he heard a voice behind him. It was the Syndicate's caretaker, Noakes. Noakes' job was to look after the building and make sure that everything there was working properly.

'Good afternoon, Noakes,' Roope said. 'I was looking for Dr Bartlett. I wanted to leave a report with him. But he's in Banbury this afternoon. Perhaps I could leave the report with someone else. Is Mr Ogleby here, or Mr Martin, or Mrs Height?'

'No, sir,' Noakes replied. 'I don't think that any of them is here this afternoon. The only graduate who might still be in the building is Mr Quinn. His car is in the car park at the back of the building.'

Roope and Noakes went to the door of Quinn's office and looked inside. Quinn's green jacket was hanging on the back of a chair and the drawers of one of his filing cabinets[17] was open. There was a note on *his* desk too.

'Quinn's jacket is still here,' Roope said. 'He can't be far away.'

'That note must be for his secretary,' said Noakes. 'Doctor Bartlett doesn't mind people going out for an hour or two. But he says that they must leave a note about where they've gone. If anybody needs to contact them urgently, we have to know where to find them.'

'Well, have any of the others left a note?' said Roope. 'Where are they?'

'I've no idea about that, sir,' said Noakes. 'But they aren't in the building. I'm going upstairs now to make a cup of tea. Would you like one?'

'No, thanks,' said Roope. 'I have to go. I'll just leave this envelope on Dr Bartlett's desk. He'll see it when he comes back from Banbury.'

Roope went back into Bartlett's office and Noakes walked towards the stairs.

4

A Body Is Found

It was 10.15 on the morning of Tuesday, 25th November. Chief Inspector Morse was at home. Morse was a very clever detective and he'd often solved difficult cases[18]. But recently he'd been bored with his job – there were no difficult cases to solve! So instead of going to his office at the headquarters of the Thames Valley Police in North Oxford, that morning, Morse had decided to get his hair cut.

The telephone rang. Morse's assistant, Sergeant Lewis, was calling. The sergeant had worked with Morse for many years. They'd worked on many difficult cases together, and although the inspector wasn't always kind to Lewis, the two men really liked each other very much.

'Hello, sir,' said Lewis. 'I've been trying to find you at Headquarters.'

'I'm going to get my hair cut,' said Morse crossly. 'Is there a problem?'

'Well, yes, there is,' said Lewis. 'A dead man has been

found in a house in Pinewood Close. Can you go there immediately, sir? He might have killed himself, but we don't know. Perhaps he was murdered.'

At once, Morse felt interested and excited.

'Who was the man, Lewis?' he asked the sergeant. 'And who found him?'

'His name was Nicholas Quinn, sir. He worked for the Foreign Examinations Syndicate. Quinn had a job at their headquarters, near Woodstock Road. He didn't go to work yesterday or today. His boss, Dr Bartlett, tried to phone him, but Quinn didn't answer his phone. Dr Bartlett is the Administrator of the Syndicate. He was worried. This morning, he sent one of Mr Quinn's colleagues – a man called Donald Martin – to Quinn's apartment. Mr Martin saw the body through a window and he called the police from a phone box[19].

'Martin is at Police Headquarters now, sir,' Lewis went on. 'He's making a statement about how he found Quinn – he's writing down a description of what happened.'

'Good,' said Morse. 'Make sure that Martin stays at Headquarters. I'll see him there later. I'll go to Pinewood Close now. Meet me there, Lewis.'

———

Pinewood Close was a small, quiet street with four houses. There was a garage for a car beside each house. As he turned his own car – a big red Jaguar – into the street, Morse saw a large policeman in uniform. He was standing with Lewis and a middle-aged woman outside Number One, the house at the end of the road. Morse recognized the large man – he was Constable Dickson.

Dickson and Lewis had been talking to the woman. Morse parked his car and walked over to them. Lewis introduced the woman to Morse.

'This is Mrs Jardine, the owner of the house, sir,' he said.

'Do you live here yourself, Mrs Jardine?' asked Morse.

'No,' replied the woman. 'I own several houses in this area and I rent[20] them to people. This house is divided into two apartments. Mr Quinn rented the downstairs apartment. A young married couple rent the upstairs apartment, but they've been away for the past few days.

'The police called me this morning,' Mrs Jardine went on. 'They said that a body had been found in one of my houses, so I came here at once.'

Morse asked Mrs Jardine to let him keep the keys of the house, then he told her that she could go home.

Morse and Lewis went into the house. There were stairs in front of them. On the right, there was a passage with a door at the end of it. They unlocked this door and they went into Nicholas Quinn's apartment.

Inside the sitting-room, the light was still switched on and a gas fire was burning. The dead body of a young man was lying on the carpet, in front of the fire. Near the body, on a small table, stood a bottle of sherry[21] and a wine glass. The bottle was almost full, the glass was almost empty.

The curtains were pulled together across the window. But there was a small gap between them, so that it was possible for somebody outside the house to look through the window, into the room.

Morse smelt the sherry which was left in the glass.

'This smells like cyanide[22], Lewis,' he said. 'This man was probably poisoned.' He looked carefully at Quinn's body. There was some white foam around the man's lips, and his eyes were wide open.

'It's going to be difficult to find out exactly when he died, Lewis,' Morse went on. 'The doctor will tell us what *he* thinks later. But *I* think that Mr Quinn has been dead for four or five days. He probably died on Friday or Saturday.'

Everything in the room was very clean and tidy. A small

waste-paper basket stood beside the fire, and inside the basket was a ball of paper. Morse picked it up, opened it out and read some words on it.

MR QUINN

I CAN'T FINISH CLEANING YOUR APARTMENT THIS AFTERNOON BECAUSE MY HUSBAND IS ILL. I HAVE TO GET SOME MEDICINE FOR HIM. I'LL COME BACK AFTER 6 O'CLOCK AND FINISH THE CLEANING THEN.
MRS EVANS

'It's a note from Quinn's cleaner[23],' said Morse. 'That's very interesting. But when did she write it?'

Morse and Lewis went into Quinn's small kitchen. On a table were a packet of butter, some eggs, some cheese and a piece of meat. Beside them was a receipt[24] from the Quality Supermarket. Why hadn't Quinn put this food in the fridge which stood in a corner of the room?

'I have to go to Police Headquarters now, Lewis,' said Morse. 'Please look in Quinn's fridge and make a list of all the things that you find in there.' Then he left the room. As he went to the door of the apartment, he noticed a green jacket hanging next to it.

———

Donald Martin was sitting nervously at a table in a small room at Thames Valley Police Headquarters. Morse read the statement that the man had already written.

I've known Nicholas Quinn for three months. On Monday, 24th November and Tuesday, 25th November, he didn't come to work and he didn't telephone to say that he was ill. My boss, Dr Bartlett, asked me to go to Quinn's apartment. He asked me to find out if Quinn was all right. I arrived at the house at about 9.30 a.m. I rang the doorbell, but nobody answered it. I looked through the window of Quinn's garage and I saw that his car was there. So I went round to the side of the house. The curtains were pulled together, but I could see into Quinn's sitting-room through a gap. I could see somebody lying on the floor. I called the police from a phone box in the street. Then I waited for them to arrive.

'Good, thank you,' Morse said to Martin, when he'd finished reading the statement. He asked the man a few questions about the people who worked at the Foreign Examinations Syndicate. Then he said, 'Please sign your name on this statement, Mr Martin, and then go back to the Syndicate building. Please tell Dr Bartlett that Chief Inspector Morse will be there soon.'

'What do you think happened to Quinn?' asked Martin. 'Did he kill himself?'

'Oh, no, I don't think so, Mr Martin,' replied Morse. 'He was murdered!'

———

On that same Tuesday, in an examination centre in Al-jamara, five young men were taking an English exam. One of them was Muhammad Dubal, the son of Sheikh Ahmed Dubal.

Five minutes before the end of the exam, Muhammad Dubal leant back in his chair and folded his arms. There was a smile on his face. He was looking very happy.

When the exam finished, the five young men gave their answer papers to the British teacher who was in charge of the exam. Before he put the answer papers into an envelope, the teacher quickly read through parts of them. He saw that Muhammad Dubal's paper was good – very good. It was much better than the other four papers. But the young teacher wasn't surprised. Muhammad's father was the ruler of Al-jamara, and he could afford the best education for his son.

The teacher went to the exam centre's office and handed the envelope to a secretary there. He told her to post it immediately to the Foreign Examinations Syndicate in Oxford, England.

———

By early afternoon that day, the police doctor[25] had been to the house in Pinewood Close. He'd agreed with Morse's opinion[26] that Quinn had died from cyanide poisoning. And the doctor also thought that Quinn had been dead for three or four days.

Now Chief Inspector Morse and Sergeant Lewis were at the Syndicate's headquarters. Dr Bartlett, Philip Ogleby, Donald Martin and Monica Height were all sitting quietly in the Administrator's office, looking at Morse. Martin had already told them the news about Quinn's death.

'Good afternoon,' Morse said to them. 'I'm sorry to tell you that your colleague, Mr Quinn, was murdered. My job is to find out who murdered him. We need to talk to you all immediately. My assistant, Sergeant Lewis, will question Mr Ogleby and Mr Martin. I will question Dr Bartlett and Mrs Height myself.'

Bartlett and Morse stayed in Dr Bartlett's office and the others left. Morse looked around the room and noticed a door behind Bartlett's desk.

'What's behind that door?' asked the inspector.

'It's a toilet,' Bartlett replied.

Then Morse began to ask Bartlett questions about Quinn. Bartlett told Morse about Quinn's work, and about his deafness. He told him that Quinn was very good at lip-reading.

'When did you last see Mr Quinn, sir?' asked Morse.

'I can't remember exactly when it was,' replied Bartlett. 'I saw him on Friday morning, but I'm not sure whether I saw him on Friday afternoon. I had a meeting in Banbury at three o'clock, so I left here at lunchtime. I don't remember seeing Quinn when I got back here at the end of the afternoon.'

Next, Morse questioned Monica Height. She was wearing a pretty green dress and the inspector guessed that she was about thirty-five years old. Morse liked pretty women and he thought that Monica was very attractive.

'Do her colleagues also find her attractive?' Morse asked himself. 'Was Quinn attracted to her? What about Martin? Or Ogleby? Or Bartlett?'

'May I call my daughter and tell her that I'll be late this afternoon?' Monica asked the inspector. 'She's at home today, studying for her exams.'

'Yes, of course, Mrs Height.'

'Please call me Monica.'

'How old is your daughter, Monica?'

'She's sixteen.'

'Sixteen!' said Morse in surprise. 'You don't look old enough to have a daughter of that age!'

'I married when I was very young, Inspector. But I'm divorced now.'

After Monica had phoned her daughter, Morse asked her when she had last seen Quinn.

'I'm not sure about that,' replied Monica. 'I remember seeing him on Friday morning, but I can't remember seeing him on Friday afternoon.'

'Did you like Nicholas Quinn, Mrs Height?' asked Morse.

'Yes, I did. I thought that he was a very nice man.'

'And did he like you? Did he ever ask you to go out with[27] him?'

'Well, yes, he once asked me to go for a drink and a sandwich at lunchtime. We went to the pub at the end of this road – the pub called the Horse and Trumpet. It's very nice there. You'd like it, Inspector.'

'Perhaps I'll see you there sometime, Monica,' said Morse.

'I hope so,' Monica replied. She looked at Morse and

smiled a wonderful smile. 'I do hope that we meet again. I'd like that.'

———

While Morse was talking to Dr Bartlett and Monica, Lewis was questioning Philip Ogleby and Donald Martin. But the sergeant didn't learn anything interesting from either of them. Ogleby remembered seeing Quinn on Friday morning, but not in the afternoon. Martin said that he couldn't remember seeing Quinn on Friday at all.

Later, Morse and Lewis discussed the four people they had already talked to.

'She's very pretty, sir, isn't she?' said Lewis suddenly.

'Who?' asked Morse. He pretended not to understand what Lewis meant.

'Monica Height, of course,' replied the sergeant.

Morse didn't say anything. But he was thinking about Monica's lovely face and her soft voice, and about the way she had looked at him. Yes, he liked her – he liked her very much. And he thought that she liked him too.

5

A Letter and Some Notes

Later that afternoon, Morse and Lewis searched Nicholas Quinn's office. Three metal filing cabinets stood against one of the walls, and there was a desk in the centre of the room.

Morse sat down behind the desk.

'You look through the files in those cabinets, Lewis,' he said. 'I'll look through the drawers in this desk.'

It took Lewis a long time to look through the files in the

first two filing cabinets. The files contained lots of papers about exams. Lewis looked at them all carefully, but he couldn't find anything useful. There was nothing to tell him why somebody had murdered Nicholas Quinn.

In the third filing cabinet, the sergeant found some letters addressed to George Bland. He also found some copies of letters *from* George Bland to some of the Syndics – the Syndics who set the Syndicate's English exams.

'George Bland was Quinn's predecessor, wasn't he, sir?' Lewis said.

Morse nodded. He was bored. He hadn't found anything interesting either. There was a calendar and some unsigned letters on the top of Quinn's desk. In the drawers of the desk, there were pencils and pens, rulers and scissors and a letter about some lip-reading classes at a college in North Oxford. There was also a diary with the dates of some meetings in it. Morse noticed that on the pages for the 4th, 5th and 6th of November, Quinn had written AED.

'What do you think that AED means?' he asked Lewis.

'I really don't know, sir,' the sergeant replied.

Morse leant back in his chair. He was still trying to think of a reason why Quinn had been murdered. Lewis had finished looking through the files from the third cabinet. He was putting the last file back into it when he noticed an envelope at the back of the lowest drawer. He pulled the envelope out, opened it and took a letter from it.

'I know what AED means now, sir,' the sergeant said, giving the envelope and letter to Morse. 'The AED is the Al-jamara Education Department.'

Morse looked at the envelope. It was addressed to George Bland and the words PRIVATE AND CONFIDENTIAL were written in large red letters in one corner. The letter was typed[28] on the official notepaper[29] of the Al-jamara Education Department. It was dated '3rd March'.

A L-JAMARA
E DUCATION
EPARTMENT

Friday, 3rd March

Dear George,

Best wishes to all at Oxford. Thank you for your
letter and for the entry forms in the package.
The entry forms for the summer exams must be ready
to be sent to the Syndicate's headquarters by Friday
20th - or at the very latest, by the 21st.
Our system is better now, although there's still room
for improvement, but after two or three
more years, we'll probably be perfect! Please
don't let any ideas for a new system destroy
the excellent system that we have now. Certainly this
kind of change will not help us. Please reply immediately.

Yours sincerely,

The letter wasn't signed. At first Morse didn't think that
it was very interesting. But as he gave it back to Lewis, he
looked at the calendar on Quinn's desk.

'When was that letter written, Lewis?' he asked.

'The third of March this year, sir.'

'That's very strange,' said Morse. ' "Friday the twentieth,"
it says in the letter. But *which* Friday the twentieth? The
twentieth of which month?' He looked down at the calendar
again. 'There was no Friday the twentieth in March, or April,
or May, or June, or July. *None* of those months had a Friday
on the twentieth.'

'Perhaps somebody made a mistake about the date,' said
Lewis. But Morse was staring at the letter.

'No, there was no mistake!' he said. 'This letter contains
a secret message, Lewis. Look! When you read, you start at

29

the top left and you read across the page. But if you read only the word at the *end* of each line, on the right – and read down the page – then you get a different meaning.'

Lewis studied the letter and his eyes opened wide as he read.

'YOUR – PACKAGE – READY – FRIDAY – 21ST – ROOM – THREE – PLEASE – DESTROY – THIS – IMMEDIATELY. What does this mean, sir?'

'Well, the letter tells us that George Bland was receiving secret packages from somebody in Al-jamara,' said Morse. 'But what was in them? That's what we need to find out!'

———

The next morning, Morse received the pathologist's[30] report on Nicholas Quinn's death. The pathologist's opinion agreed with the police doctor's opinion and Morse's own opinion. The report said that Quinn had died from cyanide poisoning. And it said that, when Quinn's body had been found, he had been dead for more than 70 hours but less than 120 hours.

'The sherry that Quinn drank *was* poisoned,' Morse told Lewis. 'And only Quinn's fingerprints[31] were on the sherry bottle and the glass. Quinn didn't commit suicide – I'm sure that he didn't kill himself. But the person who killed him must have known something about poisons.

'So, Lewis – we know *how* Quinn died, but we don't know exactly *when* he died. Quinn's colleagues saw him alive on Friday morning, but nobody remembers seeing him on Friday afternoon. So next, I'm going to find out what they were all doing on Friday afternoon.'

———

First, Morse questioned Quinn's secretary, Margaret Freeman. Margaret had been George Bland's secretary before Bland went to Al-jamara. But she'd liked Quinn much better than Bland. She was very upset about his death.

Margaret remembered that Quinn had given her some letters to type on the previous Friday morning. She'd finished them early on Friday afternoon and she'd put them on the desk in Quinn's office. Quinn wasn't in the office when she took the letters in, but his green jacket was hanging on the back of his chair.

'Mr Quinn had left a note for me,' she told Morse. 'I can't remember *exactly* what it said. But it said something about "going out" and "coming back soon". I had to leave the building in the middle of the afternoon, so I didn't see Mr Quinn again.'

When Margaret Freeman had gone, Morse sat thinking about this note. Why wasn't it still on Quinn's desk? Had Quinn thrown it into the waste-paper basket? Perhaps he had. But the waste-paper basket was empty now – the office cleaner must have emptied it.

Two large black plastic bags of waste paper were standing outside the back door of the building. Morse told Lewis to search through the bags and look for the note which Quinn had left for Margaret Freeman.

Lewis searched carefully, but he couldn't find the note. However, he did find some other notes – notes from Bartlett to all the Syndicate staff. The notes were about a fire drill[32] on the 21st November.

FIRE DRILL

THE FIRE ALARM BELL WILL RING AT 12 P.M. ON FRIDAY, 21ST NOVEMBER. WHEN YOU HEAR THE ALARM BELL, YOU MUST STOP WORKING. YOU MUST TURN OFF ALL FIRES AND LIGHTS, AND CLOSE ALL WINDOWS AND DOORS. THEN YOU MUST LEAVE THE BUILDING BY THE FRONT ENTRANCE. NOBODY IS TO REMAIN INSIDE THE BUILDING FOR ANY REASON.

T G BARTLETT (ADMINISTRATOR)

'That fire drill happened last Friday morning,' Morse said, when Lewis showed him the notes. 'So if Nicholas Quinn was at the fire drill, he was still alive at twelve o'clock.'

Morse went to Dr Bartlett's office immediately. Bartlett was talking to Monica Height. She smiled at Morse while he told the Administrator what he wanted to know. Bartlett opened a drawer, and he showed the inspector a list of all the people who worked in the Syndicate building. All their names, including Quinn's, had ticks beside them. So all these people had been at the fire drill on Friday morning.

'I don't remember seeing Quinn outside the building,' said Bartlett. 'But the list was on a chair outside the front entrance. Everybody put a tick by their own name as they came out. So Quinn must have been at the fire drill.'

'But, Inspector,' said Monica Height suddenly, 'have you talked to Noakes, the caretaker? Noakes told me this morning that Quinn was in this building late on Friday afternoon.'

'Really?' said Morse. 'I'd better find Noakes at once.'

A few minutes later, the inspector was talking to the caretaker. Noakes told him that he'd gone into Quinn's office on the previous Friday afternoon at about 4.30. He'd seen that one of the drawers of a filing cabinet was open, and that Quinn's green jacket was on the back of his chair.

'We saw a note on Mr Quinn's desk as well,' Noakes said.

'You said "we", Mr Noakes,' said Morse. 'Who did you mean by that?'

'Mr Roope was with me,' replied Noakes. 'He'd come to give a report to Dr Bartlett. But Dr Bartlett wasn't here, so Mr Roope was looking for somebody else to give the envelope to. We looked in all the offices, but we couldn't find anybody.'

Morse was very surprised by the caretaker's information. Bartlett had gone to Banbury, he'd known that. But where had all the others gone? Quinn, Monica, Martin and Ogleby, the secretaries – *all* of them had been out of the office!

'Hadn't any of the others left a note to say where they were?' he asked Noakes.

'No, sir.'

'Did you see any of them later in the afternoon?'

'Well, I saw Mr Quinn leave in his car.'

'What!' said Morse. He was very surprised now. 'You saw Mr Quinn leave? Are you sure?'

'Yes, sir. Well, I didn't see Mr Quinn himself. But I saw his *car* leave, at about ten to five.'

When Noakes left the room, Morse spoke to Lewis.

'Lewis, I want you to go and talk to the woman who cleaned Quinn's apartment – what was her name?'

'Mrs Evans,' said Lewis. 'But what shall I ask her about?'

Suddenly Morse was cross.

'Just find out everything that she knows about Quinn!' he shouted. 'You should *know* what to do, Lewis! I can't help you all the time!'

_____

When Mrs Evans opened her front door and saw Sergeant Lewis, she knew why he had come.

'You've come about Mr Quinn, haven't you, Sergeant?' she said.

'Yes,' replied Lewis. 'What can you tell me about him?'

'Not very much. I always cleaned the ground-floor apartment at Number One, Pinewood Close when Mr Quinn was out at work,' Mrs Evans explained to Lewis. 'I didn't see him very often.

'Most weeks, I cleaned Mr Quinn's apartment between three and five o'clock on Friday afternoons,' she went on. 'But last Friday, my husband was ill and he needed some medicine. So I left Mr Quinn's apartment at about four o'clock and went to get the medicine. Then I went home and made tea for my husband. I went back to Mr Quinn's apartment at quarter past six. I finished the cleaning then. I was there for about half an hour.'

'You wrote a note to Mr Quinn when you left at four o'clock, didn't you?' asked Lewis.

'Yes. I wanted to tell him why I hadn't finished the cleaning earlier.'

'Did you see Mr Quinn when you went back at quarter past six?'

'No, I didn't. But he'd left a note for *me*.'

'He left *you* a note! What did it say, Mrs Evans?'

'I can't remember exactly. It said something about going to the shops.'

'So you left a note for Mr Quinn at four o'clock. And when you got back at quarter past six, Mr Quinn had left you a note? Are you sure that the note *was* for you, Mrs Evans?'

'Oh, yes. It had my name on it.' She replied. 'Wait a minute, Sergeant, I've probably still got it. I put it in the pocket of my skirt.'

Mrs Evans went into her bedroom and came back a few minutes later with a small piece of paper. Lewis read it.

Mrs E
I'm going out for some
shopping. I'll be back
soon.
N Q

'The Quality Supermarket is very near the house,' Mrs Evans said. 'It's open till nine o'clock on Friday evenings. Mr Quinn probably went there for his shopping.'

Five minutes later, Lewis thanked Mrs Evans and went back to Police Headquarters. At last he had something important to tell Morse. The inspector was going to be very pleased with him!

6

Lies and More Lies

While Lewis was asking Mrs Evans about Quinn, Morse had gone to the Horse and Trumpet – the pub near the Syndicate building. He was drinking a glass of beer when Monica Height walked into the bar. Monica bought herself a drink, then she saw Morse. She seemed nervous.

'I know that you're asking everybody where they were last Friday afternoon, Inspector,' she said. She stopped. She looked embarrassed. But then she went on, 'Well, I was with Donald Martin. We were making love at my house.'

'Were you, Mrs Height?' said Morse coldly. 'But Mr Martin is married, isn't he?'

'Yes,' said Monica sadly. 'Do you want me to tell you about my affair with Donald?'

'No, thank you,' replied Morse. 'Excuse me, I have to go now.'

Morse finished his beer and he walked quickly out of the pub. He was feeling jealous and angry. He was angry with himself for feeling jealous. He'd only known Monica Height for one day, and it was stupid to feel jealous of Donald Martin. He was angry with himself, but he was angry with Monica too. He was angry because he was sure that she had just told him a lie.

Lewis was waiting for Inspector Morse at the Syndicate building that afternoon. The sergeant showed the inspector Quinn's note to Mrs Evans. But Morse didn't seem very pleased or excited about it.

'I thought that you'd be pleased about this note, sir,' Lewis said.

'I *am* pleased, Lewis,' said Morse. 'The note is very interesting. But there are some more important things that we don't know about yet.'

'You mean that I didn't ask Mrs Evans the right questions,' said Lewis sadly. 'Perhaps I can get some more information from her. I'll go back and talk to her again.'

'No, don't do that,' said Morse. 'We have a lot of work to do here first. Go and see if Donald Martin is back from his lunch. If he is, tell him to come and see me.'

———

Morse and Lewis sat listening to Donald Martin's story. Martin was a thin, unattractive young man with large spectacles.

'How could Monica have an affair with a man like Martin?' Morse asked himself.

Martin told the policemen that on Friday 21st November, he and Monica had left the Syndicate building at lunchtime. They'd gone to Monica's house and they'd made love there. He'd stayed with Monica until about quarter to four. Then he'd gone home to his wife.

'Why did you leave Mrs Height's house at that time?' asked Morse.

'Because Monica's daughter, Sally, usually gets home from school at about quarter past four,' said Martin. 'We didn't want her to find me there.'

'Are you in love with Mrs Height?' asked Morse coldly.

'I don't know,' replied Martin. 'Listen, is it necessary to tell everybody about my affair with Monica? We've tried to keep it a secret. I don't want my wife to find out about it.'

Martin was looking very worried, but Morse didn't try to help him. He didn't feel sorry for Martin and he didn't reply.

When Martin had gone, Morse telephoned Constable Dickson at Police Headquarters. He told Dickson to go to Monica's house and ask Sally, Monica's daughter, some questions. Then he turned to Sergeant Lewis.

'What do you think, Lewis?' he said. 'Are Monica Height and Donald Martin telling the truth about where they were last Friday afternoon?'

'Yes, sir, I think so. Don't *you* believe them?'

'No, I don't. *I* think that they are liars. Now please go and bring Philip Ogleby here. I want to talk to him.'

———

Morse hadn't spoken very much to Philip Ogleby the previous day, but he'd liked the man. Now, he asked him a lot of questions. Ogleby explained carefully to Morse about the Syndicate's work with exams for foreign countries. Morse was very interested.

'Tell me about the security[33] for the exam papers,' Morse said. 'Would it be easy for someone to steal the question papers and make copies of them?'

'No, that would be very difficult,' replied Ogleby.

'Well, I'm sure that Dr Bartlett is very careful about security,' said Morse.

Ogleby was silent for a few moments. Then he replied, 'Oh, yes. Bartlett's a very *careful* man.'

Morse looked at Ogleby. Why had he answered the question about Bartlett so strangely? Perhaps he *didn't* think that Bartlett did his job well!

'How does the exam system work, Mr Ogleby?' asked Morse.

'The questions for each subject are written here in Oxford,' Ogleby said. 'They are written by the Syndics who are experts in that subject and by the graduate here who is an expert in the subject. The Syndics and the graduate work together. The question papers are printed in Oxford, and then they're sent to the Education Departments in the foreign countries. Before the examinations take place, the papers are sent from the Education Departments to the heads of the exam centres. The centres are the schools where students take the exams.'

'But how do you know that the heads of the exam centres are honest?' asked Morse. 'They could make copies of the exam papers and sell them to the students who are going to take the exams. If they did that, the students could prepare their answers before the exams.'

'No, it's impossible, Inspector,' said Ogleby. 'The exam centres are all checked every year. We keep records of the centres and their heads. We keep records of the grades of all their students. We watch carefully for any changes in those grades. We would know at once if something was wrong.'

'Does George Bland check the centres in Al-jamara?'

'Yes, he does. But that's only one part of his job. He's in charge of the public examination system there.'

'I understand,' said Morse. 'And after the exams, the answer papers are sent back to Oxford. Then they're sent to examiners who mark them and give them grades. How do you know that those examiners are honest? Could *they* give weak students high grades if they were paid to do it?'

'No, that's also impossible,' replied Ogleby. 'We check the examiners very carefully too. We have several examiners who check the other examiners' work!'

'Well, what about here in the Syndicate building?' Morse went on. 'Would it be possible for somebody – a cleaner, for example – to take exam papers from a filing cabinet and copy them?'

'Yes, *that* might be possible,' answered Ogleby. 'But a cleaner wouldn't understand how our system works. They'd have to know which question papers were the right ones to copy. And they *wouldn't* know that. The papers are prepared in a very complicated way. They have special marks and numbers on their pages for security.'

'But what if a Syndic or one of the graduates here wanted to sell exam papers?' Morse asked.

'Oh, if a Syndic or a graduate was dishonest, it would be very easy for them make copies of the question papers,' replied Ogleby. 'But why are you asking me all these questions, Inspector?'

'Well,' said Morse, 'we have to try to find out why Mr Quinn was murdered. Perhaps he discovered that somebody here was selling exam papers. Perhaps that person was afraid that Quinn would tell other people. Perhaps he or she murdered Quinn before he *could* tell anybody.'

Suddenly Morse smiled. 'Thank you, Mr Ogleby,' he said. 'Your information is very helpful. I don't need to ask you any more questions.'

Ogleby stood up to leave, but then Morse said, 'Oh, there is one last question, sir. Where were you last Friday afternoon?'

'I went out for lunch and I didn't get back here until about half-past three,' said Ogleby. 'Then I stayed here in the Syndicate building for the rest of the afternoon.'

'Are you sure about that, sir?' asked Morse in surprise.

'Yes, Inspector. Why do you ask?'

'Two other people were here at about 4.30 on Friday afternoon,' Morse said. 'They've told me that there was nobody else in the Syndicate building at that time. They said that everyone else had left.'

Ogleby did not look worried.

'Then those two people have made a mistake,' he said. 'Or

40

perhaps they're telling lies!'

After Ogleby left the room, Morse sat alone, thinking. Noakes and Roope had been very sure that nobody else was in the Syndicate building at 4.30 on Friday afternoon. But Ogleby had said that *he* was there, and Ogleby had seemed honest. Somebody was lying. Who was it? Noakes and Roope? Or Ogleby? Was *everyone* lying?

———

Constable Dickson rang the doorbell of Monica Height's house. After a moment, an attractive young girl opened the door.

'Good afternoon, miss,' said Dickson politely. 'Is your mother here?'

'No,' replied Sally Height. 'But please come in. Do you want to ask me some questions about Mr Quinn?'

'Why aren't you at school today, miss?' asked Dickson.

'I've had exams every morning this week,' said Sally. 'But we don't have exams in the afternoons. The teachers let us go home to study in the afternoons.' Then she laughed and said, 'But I'm not doing much studying. I'm watching TV instead!'

Constable Dickson remembered his instructions from Morse. He remembered what Morse had told him to ask Sally.

'What programmes do you watch?' he asked.

'Well, there are lots of children's programmes on the TV during the afternoon. They're often very good.'

'Yes,' said Dickson. 'I saw a good children's film last Friday afternoon. It was about a dog. Did *you* see it?'

'Yes,' said Sally, smiling happily. 'I was at home then too. I *did* see it. It was wonderful, wasn't it?'

'Well, thank you for talking to me, miss,' said Dickson, 'I'd better go now.'

———

When Dickson told Morse about his conversation with Sally, the inspector felt very sad. When they'd first met, he'd liked Monica Height very much, and he'd thought that she liked him. But then he'd found out that she was already having an affair with Donald Martin. And now he knew that she'd lied to him. He knew that Monica and Martin hadn't been at her house on Friday, because Sally had been there all afternoon, watching TV.

'Monica lied to me,' thought Morse. 'And Martin lied. Perhaps Ogleby lied as well. Where were they all last Friday afternoon?'

7

The Ticket

That evening, Morse was sitting alone in his office at Police Headquarters. On the desk in front of him was a blue plastic bag, containing all the things which had been found in the pockets of Nicholas Quinn's green jacket.

He opened the bag and emptied the things out onto his desk. There was a wallet[34], a small diary, some money, two black pens, a letter from Quinn's bank, and one half of a brown paper ticket.

Morse started to write a list of these things. Then he stopped and looked carefully at the piece of ticket.

At first, the letters and numbers on the piece of ticket hadn't meant anything to him. But suddenly, he understood that the large letters were the second half of the name of a cinema in Walton Street – STUDIO 2. Quickly, Morse found a copy of the local[35] newspaper, the *Oxford Mail*, and he opened it at the page with the cinema information. He found the advertisement for STUDIO 2 and read it.

STUDIO 2 is showing the Swedish film, **Passion in the Afternoon**, for another week. The star of this adult film is the popular and sexy Inga Nielsson.

Morse phoned the cinema and explained to the manager that he was a police detective. He told the man that he was trying to get some information about a cinema ticket.

'The ticket is brown,' he said. 'And there's a number on it – 93550. Can you tell me which film performance this ticket was for?'

'Yes, sir,' the manager replied. 'When a customer buys a ticket to see a film, we tear the ticket in half. The customer keeps one half of the ticket and we keep the other half here. You've told me the colour and the number of your ticket, so I can check it with the halves that we have here. Then I'll be able to give you the information that you want. I'll need a few minutes.'

The manager went away to get the information.

A few minutes later he was speaking to Morse again.

'That ticket was for a performance of *Passion in the Afternoon* at 1.30 p.m. last Friday,' he said. 'The brown tickets are for seats at the back of the cinema. The first brown ticket which was sold for that performance was Number 93543. Your ticket is 93550. So somebody must have bought it a few minutes after the ticket office opened.'

Morse put down the phone. So Quinn had gone to the cinema last Friday afternoon to watch a sexy Swedish film. But had he gone there alone? And if not, who was with him?

———

On the Thursday afternoon, Morse visited the college where the Dean of the Foreign Examinations Syndicate taught. The Dean gave the detective tea in his comfortable rooms.

The Dean was sixty-five years old and he was going to leave the Syndicate soon. He was very upset about Quinn's death. There had never been any problems at the Syndicate before. Now it might lose its good reputation[36] because a murder had taken place at its headquarters.

'Did you think that the Syndicate building was a happy place?' Morse asked the Dean.

'Oh, yes,' said the Dean. 'Very happy.'

'Did all the Syndics and graduates like each other?'

'Well —' said the Dean, 'of course there are always *some* problems. There are sometimes problems between the older generation – people of my age – and the younger generation.'

'Are you thinking of any special problems, sir?' asked Morse.

'Perhaps,' the Dean replied carefully. 'The Administrator – Dr Bartlett – and Christopher Roope – the youngest member of the Syndicate – don't always agree with each other. For example, it was Roope who wanted us to appoint Quinn. Dr Bartlett didn't want Quinn to get the job. But Roope made the other Syndics agree with him, so Quinn *did* get the job.'

'And Bartlett wasn't very happy about that?' Morse asked. 'Are Bartlett and Roope enemies?'

'I'm sorry, I don't think that I can tell you anything more about that,' said the Dean. 'You must ask them yourself.'

———

That evening, Constable Dickson showed Sergeant Lewis a short article in the *Oxford Mail*.

Murder Investigation – Latest News

Police are investigating the murder of Mr Nicholas Quinn, of 1 Pinewood Close, whose body was found on Tuesday morning by a colleague from the Oxford Foreign Examinations Syndicate. Anyone who saw Mr Quinn on the evening of Friday 21st November, or on Saturday 22nd November, should call Chief Inspector Morse of the Thames Valley Police.

Next to the article, there was a photo of Quinn.

Lewis drove to the Quality Supermarket, near Quinn's apartment in Pinewood Close. Lewis showed the newspaper article to the supermarket manager. And he showed him the receipt which had been found with the food on Quinn's kitchen table.

When the manager looked at the receipt, he said that the things had been bought between 5.00 and 6.30 on the previous Friday evening. But he didn't recognize the man in the photo. He couldn't remember ever seeing Quinn. None of the women who worked in the supermarket could remember Quinn either.

The next morning, Morse was thinking about Christopher Roope. He hadn't talked to the young man yet, but he was becoming very interested in Roope, for several reasons.

First, he had learnt that Roope had worked in the Middle East for two years before coming to teach at Oxford University. Perhaps Roope had made dishonest arrangements with people in Al-jamara.

Second, Roope taught Chemistry at Christ Church College, so he certainly knew about poisons. He would know that cyanide killed people very quickly!

Third, Roope had visited the Syndicate's headquarters on the previous Friday afternoon. He'd told Noakes that he'd come to leave a report for Bartlett. But what had he *really* gone to the Syndicate building for? Why had he looked into all the offices? And what had he done after Noakes had gone upstairs for tea?

Fourth, Roope and Bartlett didn't like each other. Was there a special reason for that? And why had Roope wanted Quinn to get the job at the Syndicate?

Morse picked up his phone and called Roope's number at Christ Church College.

———

At just after twelve o'clock, Morse was waiting for Roope in a pub near Christ Church College. He was drinking a glass of beer when three young men came into the bar. They all had long hair and they were all wearing T-shirts and jeans.

One of the young men walked over to Morse.

'Chief Inspector Morse?' he said. 'I'm Christopher Roope. Would you like another beer?'

As Morse and Roope drank beer together, Morse asked the young man some questions about the previous Friday afternoon. Roope told the same story as Noakes, the caretaker.

'I arrived at the Syndicate building at about 4.25 to give a report to Bartlett,' he said. 'Bartlett wasn't there, and none of the graduates were in their offices. But I think that Quinn was somewhere not far away,' said Roope. 'There was a note on his desk and his jacket was on the back of a chair. And a drawer in one of his filing cabinets was open.'

'What about Mr Ogleby?' asked Morse. 'Was he in the building?'

'I didn't see him,' replied Roope. 'He certainly wasn't in his office.'

Morse nodded. He believed Roope. Then he said, 'Please tell me what you were doing for the whole of last Friday, sir.'

'Of course,' answered Roope. 'I took an early train to London. I had a meeting with a publisher there. I left the publisher's offices at about quarter to twelve, had lunch in a café, and visited a museum. Then I took the 15.05 train back to Oxford.'

Morse was sure that Roope was lying about something. The young man was talking quickly and easily. He didn't have to think about his story. He was like an actor in a play.

'Can you prove that all this is true?' asked Morse quietly. 'Did you meet anybody that you knew in London?'

Roope looked angry.

'What do you mean?' he asked. 'I told you, I went to meet a publisher there.'

'Yes, but after that,' said Morse. '*Did* you take the 15.05 train to Oxford? Perhaps you took an *earlier* train. Perhaps you were back in Oxford by lunchtime.'

'I'm telling you the truth, Inspector!' said Roope. 'Why don't you believe me?' Suddenly he smiled. 'Wait a minute,' he said. 'Perhaps I *can* prove that I caught the 15.05 train last Friday. When I got back to Oxford, it was raining heavily. So I took a taxi from the station to the Syndicate building. I'm sure that the taxi driver will remember me. I gave him a large tip! Let's go to the station now. We'll try to find him!'

A long queue of taxis was parked outside Oxford railway station. But Roope couldn't find the taxi driver who had taken him to the Syndicate building the previous Friday. Then Roope had another idea.

'When I took the train from London last Friday, I travelled in a first-class compartment,' he told Morse. 'But I'd only paid for a second-class ticket. So when I arrived here, I talked to the ticket collector. I tried to pay the extra money. Perhaps the ticket collector will remember me.'

The two men went into the station and Roope spoke to a ticket collector.

'Do you remember me?' he asked. 'Were you here last Friday afternoon?'

'No, I don't remember you,' the man answered. 'But I wasn't working last Friday.'

'Do you know who *was* working last Friday afternoon?' asked Roope.

'No, I don't know,' the man replied. 'You'll have to ask somebody in the station office. But it's lunchtime now. The office is closed.'

'Don't worry, Mr Roope,' said Morse. 'We'll find your taxi driver and the ticket collector another time. Goodbye for now.'

Roope walked away towards his college and Morse got into a taxi. He told the driver to take him to the headquarters of the Foreign Examinations Syndicate.

8

When Did Quinn Die?

In the taxi, Morse thought about Monica Height again. Monica and Donald Martin had lied to him. They hadn't been at Monica's house last Friday afternoon. But what *had* they been doing, and why were they lying about it?

Morse now thought that he knew where they had been, but he had to prove it. So he made a plan.

When he got back to the Syndicate building, he found Lewis in Quinn's office.

'Lewis, I'm going to tell Monica Height that we want to ask her some more questions,' the inspector said. 'I'll bring her here. Talk to her. Keep her here for ten minutes, while I go and look for something in her office.'

Morse quickly found Monica and brought her into Quinn's office. As Lewis started asking her questions, Morse walked to the door.

'Excuse me, I have to ask Dr Bartlett something,' he said. 'I'll be back soon.'

Morse went immediately into Monica's office and closed the door behind him. He searched the pockets of her jacket, then he searched the drawers in her desk. Monica's handbag was in one of the drawers. Morse took it out and opened it. Inside it, he found a wallet. He opened the wallet and there it was – the thing that he had been looking for! It was one half of a cinema ticket. It was half of a brown ticket for a seat at the back of Studio 2. The number on the ticket was 93556.

Morse went back into Quinn's office, where Lewis was still questioning Monica. As the inspector entered the room, Monica stopped talking and looked at him.

'Why did you lie to me about last Friday afternoon, Mrs Height?' Morse asked her.

'What do you mean?' asked Monica.

Morse showed her the cinema ticket. 'I found this in your wallet,' he said. 'You weren't at your house with Mr Martin, were you? You were at the cinema!'

Monica's face went very pale. She didn't say anything.

'Now, tell me the truth,' said Morse.

'All right,' said Monica unhappily. 'I *did* lie to you. But it's true that I was with Donald Martin last Friday afternoon. We couldn't go to my house because Sally was there. So we decided to go to the cinema. We went to see that Swedish film – *Passion in the Afternoon*. We arrived at the cinema separately and we bought tickets separately. We sat together at the back of the cinema, and I went home immediately after the film finished.'

When Monica had told her story, Morse said, 'OK, Lewis, go and get Mr Martin. Let's hear his story too.'

Lewis went out and returned a few minutes later with Donald Martin.

'Donald,' said Monica quickly, 'please tell Inspector Morse the truth now. He knows where we really were last Friday afternoon.'

Martin told Morse the same story as Monica. He said that he'd gone home immediately after the film too.

'Perhaps you'll be surprised to learn that one of your colleagues from the Syndicate was also at Studio 2 on Friday afternoon,' Morse said.

Neither Monica or Martin spoke. Monica looked unhappy but she did not look surprised.

'Yes,' continued Morse. '*Quinn* was in the cinema with you. He was sitting in the same part of the cinema as you were – at the back. Didn't you see him?'

Now Monica and Martin were staring at Morse in complete astonishment. Now, they were so surprised that they couldn't say anything.

———

'*Please tell Inspector Morse the truth now.*'

After Monica and Martin had gone, Morse laughed happily. But Lewis was very quiet.

'What's the matter, Lewis?' said Morse at last.

'Well, sir —' Lewis stopped, but after a moment he continued. 'They didn't tell us everything that they know – I'm sure about that. I think that they're still lying about something. When you said that one of their colleagues was in the cinema with them, they didn't seem very surprised. But when you told them that the colleague was Quinn, they were completely astonished. Why, sir? If they saw Quinn there, why were they so surprised by your words?'

Morse nodded slowly.

'Yes, you're right, Lewis. So perhaps *another* of their colleagues was in the cinema too. Bartlett was on his way to Banbury. It can't have been him. So that only leaves – Ogleby. Was Ogleby at the cinema too? We'll soon find out. Go and bring Ogleby here, Lewis.'

———

Philip Ogleby was looking very ill and tired when he came into the room with Lewis.

'Mr Ogleby,' began Morse. 'You told me that you were in the Syndicate building last Friday afternoon. Are you sure about that?'

'Yes, quite sure,' replied Ogleby.

'But *I* think you were in the Studio 2 cinema in Walton Street on Friday afternoon,' said Morse.

'No, you're wrong,' replied Ogleby. 'I went to Walton Street after work because my house is there. But I didn't go to the cinema at any time on Friday.'

'OK,' said Morse. 'On Friday afternoon, at about 4.30, Mr Roope was in the Syndicate building. Were you there then?'

'Oh, yes,' said Ogleby at once. 'I heard Roope talking to Noakes, the caretaker.'

Morse's eyes opened wide. This was very surprising!

'But you weren't in your office,' he said. 'How could you hear Roope and Noakes talking?'

Ogleby didn't reply. Morse waited for a moment. Then he started to talk again.

'Did you enjoy that film, *Passion in the Afternoon*, sir?'

Ogleby didn't get angry. He answered Morse quietly.

'I didn't see the film, Inspector. I didn't see it on Friday or at any other time.'

'Did you keep your ticket?'

'I didn't *have* a ticket. I wasn't at the cinema and I didn't see the film.'

———

When Ogleby had gone, Morse decided to talk to Dr Bartlett about some of the things that he'd found out that afternoon. Perhaps Bartlett could give him some helpful information.

First, he told Bartlett that all the graduates had left their offices when he was away in Banbury the previous Friday. Morse told him that Monica and Martin had gone to the cinema and that Ogleby was probably in the cinema too. And he told the Administrator about Ogleby.

'Mr Ogleby says that he was in the Syndicate building at 4.30, but Roope and Noakes said that he wasn't there.'

'I'm not really surprised about Monica and Donald Martin,' Bartlett said. 'Monica's an attractive woman and Martin's marriage isn't very happy. But I'm very surprised about Ogleby.'

'Why? Isn't he interested in sexy films?'

'I don't know about that,' Bartlett replied. 'But Ogleby never tells lies. If he *was* at the cinema, he'd tell you about it. Why should he lie?'

'I don't know,' said Morse. 'But now I need to know more about how your office works, Dr Bartlett. Can we have a long talk about that soon? There are lots of things that I want to ask you.'

'Certainly, Inspector,' said Bartlett. 'Why don't you come and have a meal with us this evening? My wife's a very good cook.'

'Thank you,' said Morse. 'I'll enjoy that very much.'

———

Late that afternoon, Morse was sitting alone in his office at Police Headquarters. There were still two hours before he had to go to dinner at Dr Bartlett's house, and he was using the time to think about the case.

There were two lists on the desk in front of him. One was the list which Lewis had made of the food in Quinn's fridge. The other was a list of the things which had been bought at the Quality Supermarket on the previous Friday evening.

Morse studied the two lists carefully. He noticed something strange. Quinn had bought butter from the supermarket that evening. But he already had plenty of butter in his fridge.

'Well, perhaps he wanted some extra butter,' thought Morse. But he didn't really believe this. He thought that the extra butter was important. And then he thought of something else. The gas fire had been burning in Quinn's room when the body was found. You had to light that kind of fire with a match. But there were no matches near the fire or in Quinn's pockets. That was very strange!

'Perhaps Quinn *didn't* return to Pinewood Close late on Friday,' thought Morse. 'Perhaps he was murdered earlier that day. Did somebody else go into his apartment during the afternoon, light his fire, leave a note for his cleaner and go out to the supermarket? Did he or she put Quinn's body there *later* – after Mrs Evans had left for the second time? Perhaps. But who could have done that? Monica? Martin? Ogleby? Roope? Or even Bartlett?'

Morse knew that Oxford was full of clever people. Quinn's

murderer was certainly very clever. It was going to be difficult to catch him or her. But Morse was clever too!

There was a handwriting expert at Police Headquarters – a man called Peters. Peters was very good at his job, and he never made mistakes.

Morse called Peters to his office and showed him two pieces of paper. The first was a report which Morse had taken from Quinn's office. Quinn had certainly written it himself. The second was the note that had been left in Quinn's apartment for Mrs Evans.

'I want to know if the report and the note were written by the same person,' Morse said. 'Please check them.'

Peters took the report and the note and left the room. A few minutes later, he came back again.

'Well?' asked Morse.

'The same person wrote the report and the note,' Peters said. 'The handwriting is exactly the same.'

'So my idea was wrong,' thought Morse. 'Quinn was still alive last Friday afternoon. He got home just after five o'clock and he wrote a note for his cleaner, Mrs Evans. He went out to the supermarket to do some shopping, then he came home, lit the gas fire, drank some sherry and died! That's crazy!'

9

Another Death

When Morse arrived at Dr Bartlett's house that evening, Bartlett introduced him to his wife and to a young man. The young man was wearing jeans, and he had long hair and a beard.

'This is our son, Richard,' Bartlett told Morse.

At first Richard was not very friendly. But later, as they were drinking sherry in the sitting-room before dinner, he began to talk about music. He loved music and he talked about it in a very interesting way. Morse loved music too. The two men enjoyed their conversation very much.

Morse could smell the food cooking in the kitchen and he began to feel hungry. Soon, Mrs Bartlett came into the room.

'Dinner is ready,' she said. 'Please come to the table.'

Morse and Bartlett went to the table, but Richard didn't move.

'Please come and eat, Richard,' said Mrs Bartlett.

'I'm not hungry,' said Richard, standing up. Suddenly, his face became red and angry.

'Please, Richard,' said Mrs Bartlett. 'I've cooked a lovely meal for us.'

'I don't want any food!' the young man shouted. 'How many times must I tell you, you stupid woman?' Then he walked out of the room, and a few minutes later they heard the sound of the front door shutting.

Mrs Bartlett's eyes filled with tears.

'I'm very sorry, Inspector,' she said. 'Richard has a mental illness[37]. He's like two different people. Sometimes he's very friendly and pleasant, but then the next moment he becomes angry and rude.

'We've spent thousands of pounds on treatment for him at expensive hospitals,' Mrs Bartlett went on. 'He's a patient at the Littlemore Hospital at the moment, but he doesn't stay there all the time.'

Dr Bartlett put his hand on his wife's shoulder, and said softly, 'Let's not talk about it now, my dear. The Inspector doesn't want to hear about our problems. He has his own problems to think about.'

The meal was wonderful. When they'd finished eating, Bartlett and Morse sat talking in the sitting-room. The furniture in the room was comfortable but simple.

'The Bartletts aren't rich people,' Morse thought. 'Life must be difficult for them.'

Mrs Bartlett brought the men coffee. Then the phone in the hall began to ring and she went to answer it.

'It's probably Richard,' Dr Bartlett said. 'After he's upset us, he often calls us to apologize – to say that he's sorry.'

At that moment, Mrs Bartlett came back into the room.

'The call is for you, Inspector,' she said to Morse. 'Sergeant Lewis wants to speak to you.'

Morse went into the hall and picked up the phone. Lewis had bad news. The police had been called to a house in Walton Street where they had found the body of Philip Ogleby. He had been murdered. He had been hit on the head with something large and heavy.

Morse went back into the sitting-room and quietly told the Bartletts the terrible news.

'Mr Ogleby has been murdered,' he said. 'I have to go at once. I'm sorry.'

Mrs Bartlett began to cry. Her husband walked slowly to the front door with Morse. Suddenly, Dr Bartlett looked like an old man. He was shocked and he couldn't speak.

———

When Morse arrived at Ogleby's house in Walton Street, Lewis was waiting for him. Philip Ogleby's body was lying on the carpet. Morse looked at the body quickly, then turned his head away. There was a terrible amount of blood.

'I want you to check on several things immediately, Lewis,' he said. 'First, find out where Christopher Roope and Donald Martin and Monica Height were tonight.'

'But sir,' said Lewis, 'we already know where Mrs Height was. She was here. She came to see Mr Ogleby. She was the

person who found his body. She called the police from the phone box in the street, then she fainted[38]. She was very shocked. She's in the Radcliffe Hospital now. The doctors want her to stay in hospital for the night.'

'But why was she here?' asked Morse. 'And how did she get in?'

'She said that she came to talk to Mr Ogleby about something important. She had a key to the house. She came in and she found his body.'

Morse was very surprised. Monica had a key for Ogleby's house! So Monica and Philip Ogleby must have been good friends. He hadn't guessed that.

'Lewis, go and see Roope and Martin immediately,' said Morse. 'Find out what they were doing this evening. Then come back here. Tomorrow, I want you to go to the Littlemore Hospital. Find out about Bartlett's son, Richard. He's a patient there. Find out what time he went back there this evening – if he *did* go back there this evening!'

———

Later that night, Morse and Lewis were searching through Ogleby's things.

'Look at this, sir,' said Lewis excitedly.

He'd found a small diary in the pocket of a pair of Ogleby's trousers. Most of the pages were empty, but there was a drawing on one of them. He gave the diary to Morse.

'Look, sir,' he said. 'It's a drawing of a cinema ticket!'

Morse stared at the drawing. At last he said, 'It's a drawing of the ticket that we found in Quinn's pocket! The ticket number is exactly the same!'

———

Morse was sitting in his office at 7.30 a.m. on Saturday 29th November. He was tired because he'd slept very badly. He'd been thinking about Ogleby's murder, and about the strange drawing of the cinema ticket.

Lewis had questioned Donald Martin and Christopher Roope the night before. He'd asked them where they'd been during the evening. Martin had told Lewis that he'd gone out to visit several pubs, alone. He'd gone home at about quarter to eleven. Roope had said that he was working at home all evening. He'd been alone too.

Later that morning, the Dean of the Syndicate telephoned Morse. He'd heard the terrible news about Ogleby and he was very shocked.

'I want to tell you something, Inspector,' he said. 'It's a very small thing and it may not be very important. But the murders of Quinn and Ogleby have made me remember it.'

'What is it, sir?' asked Morse.

'Well, it's about the evening when the Sheikh of Al-jamara invited us all to a dinner at his hotel. Something happened that evening. By the time that most people had gone home, it was very late. But Ogleby and Quinn were still there. Then, when Quinn left the hotel, Ogleby immediately followed him out. Perhaps they wanted to talk about something important.'

———

In the afternoon, Morse visited Monica Height in a room in the Radcliffe Hospital. She was sitting in bed, looking pale and nervous.

'Tell me what happened last night, Monica,' said Morse.

'There isn't much that I *can* tell you, Inspector,' replied Monica sadly. 'I went to Philip's house at about half-past eight and I found him lying dead on the carpet.'

'Did you have a key to his house?'

'Yes,' Monica said quietly. 'Philip and I were very good friends.' She was silent for a moment. Then she went on. 'You know about my affair with Donald Martin. Well, I was having an affair with Philip Ogleby too. I went into his house. It was terrible. There was blood everywhere and I didn't know what to do. I couldn't stay in the house. So I ran out into the street and I called the police from a phone box. I don't remember anything else. I must have fainted. When I woke up, I was in this hospital.'

'Why did you want to talk to Mr Ogleby last night?' asked Morse.

'He wanted to talk to *me*,' replied Monica. 'I think that he wanted to talk about Nicholas Quinn's murder.'

'Do you think that he knew something about it?'

'I don't know. But Philip was a very clever man, Inspector,' said Monica. 'I think that he *did* know something which was important. But I don't know what it was.'

Morse knew that Monica had already told him several lies. Was she lying again now? He didn't know. And he still didn't know why she had lied to him about going to the cinema with Martin. He couldn't understand it. He was silent for several minutes.

'Are you all right, Inspector?' asked Monica at last.

'Yes, I'm fine. I was thinking about something else. Sorry.'

Monica held Morse's hand tightly for a few seconds.

'Please come and see me again,' she said. 'And please take care of me.' Morse saw fear in her lovely eyes.

'I'm frightened, Inspector,' Monica said. 'I'm very, very frightened.'

———

Morse had left his Jaguar in the hospital car park. He got into it and he was just starting the engine when he saw somebody walking towards the hospital entrance. It was Donald Martin. Morse opened the passenger door[39] and shouted, 'Mr Martin! Please get into the car.'

Martin looked angry.

'I'm sorry, Inspector, I haven't got time now,' he said. 'I'm going to visit Monica.'

'Oh, no, you're not,' said Morse. 'Get into the car – now!'

10

The Exam Papers

Morse drove Donald Martin to Police Headquarters and questioned him for nearly an hour. He didn't like the man and he was not kind to him.

'How can Monica think that somebody like Martin is attractive?' he asked himself.

Martin told Morse that he had gone out the previous night, to visit several different pubs.

'I don't usually go to pubs alone,' he said, 'but I've been sleeping badly since Quinn's death. Drinking beer helps me to sleep.'

Then Morse asked Martin again about the previous Friday afternoon.

'Why did you say that you and Mrs Height were at her house?' he asked. 'Why did you lie to me? Why didn't you just tell me that you'd gone to the cinema?'

'I'm sorry, Inspector,' replied Martin. 'Yes, I *did* lie. But Monica asked me to say that we were at her house.'

Morse couldn't get any more information from Martin. But he was sure that the man was still lying to him.

———

Nigel Denniston was a teacher of English. He taught at a school in a small town in the south of England. He often earned extra money by marking English exam papers for the Foreign Examinations Syndicate. On the evening of Saturday, 29th November, Mr Denniston was sitting in his study. He opened a large package which contained exam answer papers in several envelopes.

The first envelope contained five answer papers from Aljamara. Mr Denniston pulled them out and started to mark them.

An hour later, he had marked four of the five answer papers. None of them was very good. They were full of spelling and grammar mistakes, and the students hadn't really answered the questions. Mr Denniston had written a mark at the top of each paper – 35%, 34%, 27% and 19%.

He started reading the fifth paper. Immediately he saw that it was better than the others. And it was not just better, it was very good – it was excellent. The answers were interesting and well written, with very few mistakes. Mr Denniston quickly read the paper to the end and he gave it a mark of 90%.

The name on the front of the paper was Muhammad Dubal. Denniston had never seen the name before. But whoever this student was, he was clever and he had worked very hard.

———

At the same time, George Bland was sitting alone in his apartment in Al-jamara. He was feeling sad because he was thinking about Oxford. Bland missed his life there – the university, the people, the beautiful countryside around the city. He didn't like living in Al-jamara very much. It was too hot for him, and he wasn't happy in his job at the Education Department. The people there seemed friendly, but he knew that they didn't trust him.

And now Bland had had some terrible news from Oxford. Earlier in the week, Bartlett had sent him a message about Quinn's death. And that morning, Bland had received another message – a message which *wasn't* from Bartlett.

Bland was very worried. He was worried that people were going to find out that he'd been dishonest. But he had his passport ready. It was in his wallet, together with a plane ticket. The ticket was for a flight to Zurich the following day.

When he'd finished talking to Donald Martin, Morse went back to Philip Ogleby's house.

First, the inspector went into Ogleby's bedroom. It was a simple room – there wasn't much furniture and there were no pictures on the walls. Then he went into the sitting-room. Ogleby's body and the blood-stained carpet had been taken away. There were a lot of bookshelves around the walls.

Morse took a book from one of the shelves. It was a book about the use of drugs and chemicals in medicine. A piece of paper was pushed between two of the pages. Morse opened the book at this place, and he immediately saw an article about cyanide, the poison which had killed Nicholas Quinn.

So Ogleby had been reading about cyanide. Why? Had *he* poisoned Quinn with cyanide? Or had he known about someone *else* who'd poisoned Quinn with it?

Next, Morse went to see Ogleby's doctor. The doctor gave Morse some surprising information. Philip Ogleby had been very ill. He would have died within a year.

'Did Mr Ogleby know that he was going to die soon?' Morse asked the doctor.

'Oh, yes,' the man replied. 'Ogleby always wanted to know the truth. I couldn't lie to him.'

'Did he tell anybody else about his illness?'

'I don't think so,' said the doctor. 'I don't think that he

had many friends. Ogleby liked being alone.'

'Do you think that he was planning to commit suicide? Was he going to kill himself?'

'I don't think so,' said the doctor. 'But if he *had* committed suicide, I'm sure that he would have chosen a quick and simple way of doing it. Cyanide, for example.'

Morse walked back to his Jaguar, thinking about Philip Ogleby. The man had probably been reading about cyanide because he was planning to kill himself, not because he was planning to kill his colleague, Quinn!

Morse was feeling cross. He knew that he hadn't had a very successful week. He wasn't going to solve either of the murder cases without a lot more information.

But there was one person who he wanted to talk to again – Nicholas Quinn's secretary. He was going to Margaret Freeman's home next. She was waiting for him.

Sergeant Lewis had visited the Oxford railway station and he'd spoken to drivers from four different taxi companies. At last he'd found a driver who remembered taking Christopher Roope from the station to the Syndicate building on the afternoon of Friday 21st November. Roope had given the driver a large tip – he remembered that!

Next, the sergeant had driven to the Littlemore Hospital – the hospital where Richard Bartlett was a patient. Lewis had talked to Richard's doctor there. The doctor gave him a list of all the private hospitals where Richard had received treatment for his mental illness. The young man had been receiving treatment for many years, and all the private hospitals were very expensive.

'Mrs Bartlett doesn't work,' Lewis thought. 'The Bartletts don't have much money. How do they pay for Richard's treatment?'

Morse and Lewis had arranged to meet at ten o'clock that evening in Morse's office at Police Headquarters. Lewis arrived there before Morse. He sat and waited, and at last the inspector came into the room. Lewis told Morse everything he had learnt from the taxi driver and from Bartlett's doctor. Morse listened carefully but he didn't seem very interested.

'I've got a surprise for you, Lewis,' Morse said suddenly. 'We're going to arrest someone on Monday morning.'

'But the inquest[40] on Quinn's death is on Monday morning, sir,' said Lewis.

'That's right,' said Morse. 'And the person we're going to arrest will be at the inquest. We'll do it as soon as the inquest ends.'

'Please tell me who you're going to arrest, sir.'

'No, Lewis,' said Morse, smiling. 'I want you to be surprised!'

———

When Morse had talked to Margaret Freeman, he'd asked her only one question. Margaret had thought that it was a very strange question, but Morse had been pleased with her answer. His question had been about the note that Quinn had left for her on his desk that Friday afternoon.

'We haven't found the note,' Morse had said. 'It wasn't in the plastic bags with the other waste paper. Can you tell me, did Quinn write your initials, "M.F.", at the top of that note?'

'Yes,' Margaret had replied. 'He did.'

11

An Arrest

The inquest on Nicholas Quinn's death took place on Monday morning, in the coroner's[41] courtroom in the city centre.

At eleven o'clock, most of the people who had known Quinn in Oxford were standing outside the courtroom, waiting for the inquest to start. The Dean of the Syndicate, Dr Bartlett, Monica Height and Donald Martin were standing together. Christopher Roope was staring thoughtfully at the floor. Mrs Jardine, and the cleaner, Mrs Evans, were there too.

At ten minutes past eleven, a court official called everybody into the courtroom. When they had all sat down, the coroner came into the room too.

Mrs Jardine, Donald Martin, Dr Bartlett, Sergeant Lewis and Constable Dickson stood, one after another, in the witness box – the place where people answered the coroner's questions. Each of them told the coroner what they knew about Nicholas Quinn.

Then the coroner called the police doctor to the witness box. The doctor told him that Quinn had died from cyanide poisoning.

Next, the coroner called Chief Inspector Morse.

'Are you in charge of the investigation into the death of Mr Nicholas Quinn?' he asked the detective.

'Yes, sir,' replied Morse, 'but —'

Suddenly there was a noise at the entrance to the courtroom. A young man with a beard came into the room and sat down next to Constable Dickson. It was Richard Bartlett.

'Sir,' Morse went on, 'I believe that Mr Quinn was murdered. But I need more time to finish my investigation into

Mr Quinn's death. Please, will you delay this inquest for a fortnight?'

'Have you arrested anybody for the murder yet?' asked the coroner.

'No, sir, but I'm going to arrest somebody very soon,' replied Morse.

'Very well, Chief Inspector,' said the coroner. 'I agree to delay this inquest for a fortnight.'

The coroner left the room and Morse left the witness box. The inspector walked slowly across the courtroom and stood in front of Richard Bartlett for a moment. At the back of the room, Richard's father put his hands over his face and his body began to shake. But Morse moved away from Richard without speaking and he walked on – past Mrs Evans, past Mrs Jardine, past Monica Height, past Donald

Martin and past Dr Bartlett. He stopped in front of Christopher Roope.

'Christopher Roope,' said Morse, 'I arrest you for the murder of Nicholas Quinn.'

Roope stared at Morse in astonishment and anger.

'What are you talking about, Inspector?' he said.

Sergeant Lewis and Constable Dickson walked over to them and Lewis put his hand on Roope's shoulder.

'Please come with us, sir,' he said.

'You're making a terrible mistake,' said Roope.

A moment later, the young Chemistry lecturer was walking out of the courtroom with Dickson on his right side and Lewis on his left. Everybody in the courtroom watched him go, but nobody said anything.

Morse, Lewis and Roope were sitting in a small room at Police Headquarters.

'Well, Mr Roope, do you want to tell me how you killed Nicholas Quinn?' asked Morse. 'Or shall I tell *you*?'

'You tell *me*, Inspector,' answered Roope. 'You must think that you know.'

'You arrived at the Syndicate building at about 4.25 on the afternoon of Friday 21st November,' began Morse. 'But nobody was there except for Noakes, the caretaker. You told him that you had a report to give to Dr Bartlett. You and Noakes looked in all the offices, including Mr Quinn's office, but you couldn't find anybody. It seemed that the building was empty.

'When Noakes went upstairs for his tea, you didn't leave the building,' Morse went on. 'Instead, you went back into Quinn's office. Everything in the office was exactly as you'd planned it would be.'

'I'd planned it would be?' said Roope. 'What do you mean?'

'Everything in the room would make someone think that Quinn was somewhere nearby,' said Morse. 'His green jacket was hanging on the back of a chair, and a drawer of one of his filing cabinets was open. There was even a note for his secretary on his desk. You read the note and you decided to take it with you. You thought that it might be useful.'

'Where did I take it?' asked Roope.

'To Quinn's apartment. And this is what you did next, Mr Roope,' said Morse. 'Noakes had told you that Quinn's car was in the car park at the back of the building. You put on Quinn's jacket and found his car keys in one of the pockets. You took the note from his desk, walked out through the back door of the Syndicate building, and drove his car out of the car park. Noakes saw the car leave, but he thought that Quinn was driving it.

'You drove Quinn's car to his apartment in Pinewood Close and you parked it in his garage,' Morse continued. 'Then you went into Quinn's apartment and saw the note which Mrs Evans, Quinn's cleaner, had left for him. This note contained very bad news for you. Mrs Evans had not finished cleaning and she was coming back later!

'At first, you didn't know what to do, but then you had a very clever idea. You had Quinn's note to his secretary, Margaret Freeman, with you. Her initials, "M.F.", were written at the top of this note. You changed the initials from "M.F." to "Mrs E", and you left the note in the sitting-room. When she returned, Quinn's cleaner thought that the note was for her. She thought that Quinn had come back and written the note while she had been away.

'You lit Quinn's fire with a match. Then you put the used match in your pocket,' Morse went on. 'That was a mistake. If Quinn had lit the fire himself, there would have been a used match in the room. After that, you went to the supermarket near Pinewood Close and bought some food. You took it back to the apartment and put it in Quinn's kitchen.'

'You're crazy!' said Roope. 'Why should I do all these things? Why should I wear Quinn's jacket, drive his car and buy food for him?'

'Because you wanted everybody to think that Quinn was still alive on Friday evening,' replied Morse. 'You wanted people to think that he drove home on Friday evening and killed himself that night. But Quinn was dead by the Friday afternoon. I know that now!'

There was a long silence in the room. At last, Roope spoke.

'You believe that Quinn was dead by the Friday afternoon?'

Morse nodded. Roope began to laugh.

'And you think that I murdered him?'

'Yes,' said Morse. 'Tell me the truth, Mr Roope.'

'I *have* told you the truth. I was in London that Friday,' said Roope. 'I got back to Oxford at about quarter past four. If you're right about the time of Quinn's death, I was in London when he died. *I* couldn't have murdered Quinn.'

Morse began to look worried.

The was a phone on the table in the room. Roope pointed to it.

'Can I make a call?' he asked.

'Yes,' said Morse.

Roope picked up the phone and dialled a number. He spoke to someone for a few minutes, then he gave the phone to Morse.

'Please speak to this man,' Roope said. 'It's the taxi driver who took me from the station to the Syndicate building that Friday.'

Morse spoke to the taxi driver. Then he put the phone down.

'All right, Mr Roope,' he said. 'Perhaps you *did* get a train back from London last Friday afternoon. Did you find the ticket collector too?'

'Yes I did. He was away from work when we tried to find him last week.'

'All right,' said Morse. 'So you *were* telling the truth. We must try to stop the news of your arrest appearing in the newspaper.'

He dialled the number of the *Oxford Mail* and he spoke to someone for a few minutes.

When he put the phone down, his face was red and he looked embarrassed.

'It's too late to stop the article about your arrest appearing in today's paper,' he said. 'But there'll be another article tomorrow, saying that we've made a mistake. I'm sorry, Mr Roope, mistakes do happen sometimes. Would you like Sergeant Lewis to take you home in his car?'

'No, thank you,' said Roope. 'I'll go on a bus. Goodbye!'

Roope left the room angrily.

Sergeant Lewis was very confused. Since the inquest, he'd been wanting to ask his boss several questions. Some of them were about Richard Bartlett. Morse had already known that the young man hadn't committed any crimes. And Richard hadn't even *known* Quinn. Why had the inspector asked the young man to come to the inquest? Did he want to make Dr Bartlett nervous? And another question was about the arrest of Roope. Morse had already known about the taxi driver when he'd arrested Roope. Lewis had told the inspector about the man himself. What was Morse doing?

Suddenly, Morse looked at Lewis and smiled – a big happy smile. Morse's plan was working well, but Lewis didn't know that!

_____

It was a cold, wet evening. Sergeant Lewis was sitting in a car outside Christopher Roope's house. Lewis was going to watch the house all night.

Roope was inside the house. He knew that the police were watching him. Morse had let him go this time, but Roope was sure that Morse would arrest him again.

_____

Early the next morning, a boy brought some newspapers to the house. Roope took the newspapers and he gave the boy some money and a note. He told the boy to take the note to an address in Oxford.

Later in the morning, Constable Dickson came to take Lewis's place. He sat in another car and watched the house. At about lunchtime, Roope left the house. Immediately, Dickson called Morse on the phone in the car and told him that Roope had gone out.

'Follow him, Dickson!' Morse said. 'Tell me where he goes. But don't let him see you.'

Roope walked slowly to the railway station. He sat in a café there, drinking coffee and looking out at the car park. He saw a big red Jaguar drive into the car park and he knew that it was Morse's car. He knew that Morse was watching him, so he finished his coffee and he left the café.

12

Lewis Asks Some Questions

Morse decided that it was time for him to talk to Dr Bartlett about some of his suspicions[42]. He showed Bartlett the letter to George Bland which Lewis had found in the filing cabinet in Quinn's office.

AL-JAMARA
EDUCATION
DEPARTMENT

Friday, 3rd March

Dear George,

Best wishes to all at Oxford. Thank you for your
letter and for the entry forms in the package.
The entry forms for the summer exams must be ready
to be sent to the Syndicate's headquarters by Friday
20th – or at the very latest, by the 21st.
Our system is better now, although there's still room
for improvement, but after two or three
more years, we'll probably be perfect! Please
don't let any ideas for a new system destroy
the excellent system that we have now. Certainly this
kind of change will not help us. Please reply immediately.

Yours sincerely,

'But this letter is nonsense,' said Bartlett. 'The dates in it are all wrong. The letter is dated the third of March. But the summer examination package wasn't ready until April, so how could Bland have sent it to Al-jamara before March? And the twentieth of March this year wasn't a Friday.'

'We know that, sir. The letter has a secret meaning,' said Morse. 'Read the words down the right hand side of the page.'

Bartlett read slowly.

'YOUR – PACKAGE – READY – FRIDAY – 21ST – ROOM – THREE – PLEASE – DESTROY – THIS – IMMEDIATELY.' The Administrator turned pale. 'I understand you, Inspector. This is very worrying. Do you think that George Bland was doing something dishonest with the exam papers?'

'Yes,' replied Morse. 'I think that the package that the letter speaks about was a package of money for George Bland. He was selling the exam papers for a large amount of money. He was copying and selling the papers to students, so that they knew the questions before they took their exams.'

'I'm sure that Quinn found out about the selling of the exam papers,' Morse continued. 'And he found out that somebody here in Oxford was working with Bland. I think that Quinn went to this person and told him or her what he had found out. And I think that he or she murdered Quinn before he could tell anybody else.'

'But what about Ogleby?' asked Bartlett. 'Did Ogleby find out about this person too? Was that why *he* was murdered?'

'I don't know,' said Morse. 'But perhaps the person Quinn found out about *was* Ogleby. Perhaps it was Ogleby who murdered Quinn.'

Bartlett was very shocked by what Morse had said.

'No,' the Administrator said quickly. 'I don't believe that, Inspector. Ogleby was a very honest man and he'd worked here for many years. He wouldn't have done anything to make trouble for the Syndicate. He would never have done anything to give the Syndicate a bad reputation.'

'Dr Bartlett,' said Morse. 'I want you to contact all the Syndics. Ask them to come to a meeting here in the Syndicate building at ten o'clock on Friday morning. Tell them that this meeting is very important and that they must all come.'

At 9.30 a.m. on Thursday 4th December, Roope left his house to go to work. But Lewis and Constable Dickson were waiting outside his front door. As soon as he stepped outside, they arrested him. They arrested him for the murders of Nicholas Quinn and Philip Ogleby.

That afternoon, Lewis went to see Morse in his office.

'Please, will you explain to me about Quinn's murder, sir,' said Lewis. 'There are still some things which I don't understand.'

'Of course I'll explain,' said Morse. 'Quinn's murder was a very clever crime.

'First, Lewis, I had to find out exactly *when* Quinn was murdered,' the inspector continued. 'And I now know that he was murdered at exactly twelve o'clock on Friday 21st November, in the Syndicate building.'

'How can you be so sure of that?' asked the sergeant.

'There was a fire drill at that time and everybody except Quinn and the murderer left the building as soon as they heard the alarm bell,' replied Morse. 'The murderer had invited Quinn into his office just before twelve o'clock and told him to pour himself a glass of sherry. Quinn poured the sherry. At twelve o'clock, the bell started ringing loudly for the fire drill, but Quinn couldn't hear it because he was deaf. He drank the sherry and he died almost immediately from cyanide poisoning.

'It was very easy for the murderer to take Quinn's body out through the back door of the building, into the car park,' Morse went on. 'Nobody saw him, because everybody else who worked in the building was standing outside the *front* entrance for the fire drill. The murderer hid the body in the boot[43] of Quinn's own car, then he went to join his colleagues at the fire drill. There was a list of names outside the front entrance, and the murderer put a tick next to both his own name and Quinn's name.'

'But why?' asked Lewis.

'The murderer wanted everybody to think that Quinn was still alive on Friday afternoon,' replied Morse. 'He wanted people to think that Quinn had left a note for his secretary and had gone to the cinema.

'But think about it carefully, Lewis,' Morse continued. 'Nobody remembers *seeing* Quinn at the fire drill. And nobody saw him on the Friday afternoon. Noakes saw Quinn's car driving away from the Syndicate building. But it wasn't Quinn inside it – it was somebody else.'

'Who?' asked Lewis.

'Roope,' replied Morse. 'Roope was pretending to be Quinn.'

'But, sir,' said Lewis, 'we know that Roope went to London on Friday morning. He couldn't have murdered Quinn at twelve o'clock in the Syndicate building in Oxford. He was in London at that time. Roope *can't* have been the murderer!'

'Yes, that's right,' said Morse. 'And Roope made sure that he could prove that his story was true. He tried to pay the extra money to the ticket collector at Oxford Station so that the man would remember him. He gave his taxi driver a very large tip for the same reason. But Roope didn't murder Quinn himself, Lewis. He had a partner – somebody was working with him. It was this other person who murdered Quinn. Both Roope and this other person were working with George Bland. And the three of them were making a lot of money from selling exam papers to the Sheikh. They were probably selling them to people in other countries too.'

'So what did Roope do that afternoon?' asked Lewis.

78

'I told him exactly what he'd done, when we arrested him the first time. You heard me tell him, Lewis,' Morse replied. 'Roope was at the Syndicate building on Friday afternoon, we know about that. He and Noakes looked into Quinn's office together. But when Noakes went upstairs for a cup of tea, Roope went into Quinn's office again. He put on Quinn's green jacket, and he took the note to Quinn's secretary which he found on the desk. Quinn's car keys and house keys were in the pocket of the jacket. So Roope, pretending to be Quinn, drove Quinn's car to Pinewood Close. Quinn's body was in the boot.

'When Roope got to Quinn's apartment, he found a note from Mrs Evans, Quinn's cleaner,' Morse went on. 'The note said that that she would be back later. So Roope cleverly changed the note which Quinn had written to his secretary. He changed it into a note to the cleaner. Then he lit the gas fire and went out again. He went to the supermarket and he bought some food. He'd already made one mistake – he'd not left the used match in Quinn's apartment when he lit the fire. At the supermarket, he made another mistake. Quinn already had plenty of butter, but Roope bought some more butter. When I saw the extra butter, I guessed that Quinn hadn't bought it himself.'

'When did Roope take Quinn's body into the house?' asked Lewis.

'When he came back from the supermarket, Roope waited near the house,' Morse said. 'It was dark then. He saw Mrs Evans leave. He knew that Quinn's neighbours were not in the upstairs apartment. He got Quinn's body out of the boot of the car and he pulled it into the house. He put it on the carpet in front of the gas fire in Quinn's sitting-room. On the table beside the fire, he put the bottle of sherry and the glass, which he had brought from the Syndicate building. Quinn's fingerprints were on the bottle and the glass because he'd poured the sherry into the glass himself.'

'But I still don't understand about the cinema,' said Lewis. 'If you're right about the murder, Quinn didn't go to the cinema. So Monica Height and Donald Martin *didn't* see him there. Why did they lie about going there themselves?'

'I think that they saw somebody at the cinema who they weren't expecting to see,' replied Morse. 'And that really shocked Monica. She didn't want me to find out about this person, so she lied about the visit to Studio 2, and she told Donald Martin to lie too.'

'But what about Ogleby?' asked Lewis. 'He said that he was in the Syndicate building on Friday afternoon. But Roope and Noakes didn't see him. And he drew a picture of Quinn's cinema ticket. Why? Was Ogleby at the cinema? Did Martin and Monica see *him* there?'

'No. Ogleby told us the truth,' said Morse quietly. 'He *wasn't* at the cinema that Friday afternoon. He was in the Syndicate building. But he wasn't in his own room. I think that he was hiding in the toilet behind Bartlett's desk when Roope and Noakes looked into Bartlett's office. That's why they didn't see him.'

'I'm sorry, sir,' said Lewis, 'but I still don't understand. Who *did* kill Quinn? And who killed Ogleby?'

'I'll answer all your questions at the meeting with the Syndics tomorrow morning, Lewis,' replied Morse. 'I'll explain everything then.'

———

That evening, Morse went to a lip-reading class at a local college. He found the class very interesting. He sat at the back of the room and watched the teacher. He knew that she was talking because he could see her lips moving. But no sound came out.

After the class, he talked to the teacher.

'The most difficult words to lip-read,' she told Morse,

'begin with the letters P or B or M. These words are very confusing because they look the same to somebody who is trying to lip-read. Words which begin with the letters T or D or N are also confusing, for the same reason.'

13

The Truth at Last

The next morning at ten o'clock, eleven of the twelve Syndics of the Foreign Examinations Syndicate came to the meeting in the Syndicate building. They all sat round a big table. Morse and Lewis and Bartlett were there too. But there was one empty chair at the table.

Bartlett quietly told the Syndics about the selling of the exam papers. Everybody was very shocked.

Then Morse stood up and said, 'The deaths of Mr Quinn and Mr Ogleby were the result of this problem about the exam papers. One of the people who was selling the papers was Christopher Roope. We arrested Mr Roope again yesterday, and he's at Police Headquarters now.

'Until last summer, Roope was working with your colleague, George Bland, who is now in Al-jamara,' Morse continued. 'Roope and Bland were making a lot of money from selling copies of the exam papers in Al-jamara and probably other countries too. A few weeks ago, Nicholas Quinn found out what Roope and Bland had been doing. And he learnt that Roope was *still* selling exam papers. He learnt the truth at the dinner given by the Sheikh of Al-jamara. Quinn was deaf, but he was an excellent lip-reader. He saw the Sheikh talking to Roope about the exam papers. He read Bland's name on the Sheikh's lips. But he read another person's name as well. Someone else was helping Roope too.

'Ogleby was also at this dinner,' Morse went on. 'He saw Quinn watching the Sheikh. At the end of the evening, Quinn told Ogleby what he had found out about the exam papers. Ogleby was shocked. He decided to look for proof of Quinn's story. On the afternoon of Friday 21st November, all Ogleby's colleagues were away from this building. Quinn was already dead by then – he'd been killed at twelve o'clock. But Ogleby didn't know that. During that afternoon, Ogleby searched all the offices here. He was in Dr Bartlett's office when Roope arrived. When he heard Roope coming, Ogleby hid in the toilet behind Dr Bartlett's desk. He didn't want anyone to find him in Dr Bartlett's office. He waited in the toilet. He heard Roope talking to Noakes. Then he heard someone come back into the office and quickly leave again. And later that day, Ogleby began to understand that Roope had helped the person who murdered Quinn with the crime.'

'But Roope was in London that day,' said the Dean. 'He didn't murder Quinn!'

'Roope was working with a partner. The partner was a member of the Syndicate's staff,' replied Morse. 'It was this *partner* who murdered Quinn – at exactly twelve o'clock that Friday, when the bell was ringing for the fire drill.'

The Syndics looked at each other. Who was Morse talking about? Who was Roope's partner in Quinn's murder?'

Morse nodded his head at Lewis, and Lewis got up and walked quietly to the door. A few minutes later he returned with Monica Height.

———

Everybody round the table stared at Monica in astonishment. Was *she* Roope's partner in the crime?

Morse started speaking again.

'Mrs Height,' he said, 'you told me that you were at your house with Donald Martin on the afternoon of Friday 21st

November. But later you changed your story and said that you and Mr Martin were at the Studio 2 cinema in Walton Street. Is that correct?'

'Yes,' Monica replied very quietly.

'So you lied about going to the cinema,' said Morse. 'And you asked Mr Martin to lie about it too. Will you tell me why? Perhaps you saw somebody that you knew at the cinema – somebody that you didn't want to tell me about. Is that right?'

'Yes,' said Monica.

'Do you see that person in the room now?'

'Yes.'

'Can you please point to that person?'

Monica lifted her arm and pointed. She pointed at the Administrator of the Syndicate – Dr Bartlett.

'Yes,' said Morse. 'Dr Bartlett and Christopher Roope worked together to murder Nicholas Quinn.'

———

Bartlett had been taken away to Police Headquarters. Morse and Lewis were alone in the Syndicate building. Lewis asked the inspector how he'd discovered that Bartlett was the murderer.

'The Dean told me that Roope and Bartlett didn't like each other,' replied Morse. 'They didn't agree with each other at meetings. I asked myself why not. Then I understood that Roope and Bartlett were like actors in a play. They were partners and they were working together with George Bland. But they wanted other people to think that they were enemies. That's why they always argued at meetings. If one of them wanted something to happen, the other one disagreed with him.'

'But why was Bartlett working with Roope?' asked Lewis. 'Why was he selling the exam papers?'

'Bartlett needed money,' said Morse. 'His son, Richard, is

83

very ill and he needs special medical treatment at expensive hospitals. Bartlett couldn't pay for the treatment – the Bartletts don't have much money. Dr Bartlett sold the exam papers to get money for his son.'

'So Bartlett murdered Quinn during the fire drill and put the body in the boot of Quinn's own car,' said Lewis. 'And later, Roope came here and pretended to be Quinn, so that people would think that Quinn was still alive. I understand all that. But I don't understand about the cinema. Why did Bartlett go to the cinema on Friday afternoon?'

'Because he wanted us to think that *Quinn* had gone there,' replied Morse. 'He wanted us to think that Quinn was still alive on Friday afternoon. So he went to the cinema and bought a ticket for that afternoon's film. It was a very clever plan, but it went wrong. As he was leaving the cinema, Monica Height came in. Bartlett didn't see her, but she saw *him*.

'Then Bartlett came back to the Syndicate headquarters. He knew that Roope was coming here later that afternoon – the two men had planned the crime together. So Bartlett left the cinema ticket on his own desk. Perhaps there was also a note for Roope, saying, "Put this ticket in Quinn's pocket. His keys are in his jacket." Then Bartlett went to his meeting in Banbury.'

'But what about Ogleby?' asked Lewis.

'Quinn had read Bartlett's name on the lips of the Sheikh at the dinner,' said Morse. 'When they left the hotel together, he told Ogleby that Bartlett was dishonest. At first, Ogleby couldn't believe it. He wanted to find some proof that Bartlett was selling the exam papers.

'When Bartlett was away on Friday afternoon, Ogleby began to search his office, but he couldn't find any proof. But, he saw the cinema ticket on Bartlett's desk, together with Bartlett's note to Roope. He thought that this was very strange, so he made a drawing of the cinema ticket.

'Then Ogleby heard Roope and Noakes outside the office,' Morse went on. 'He didn't want anyone to find him in Bartlett's office, so he hid in the toilet. He stayed there until Roope had returned to the room on his own and had gone away again.

'When he came out of the toilet, Ogleby saw that the cinema ticket and the note had gone from Bartlett's desk. So he knew that Roope had taken them. Later, he understood that Roope had driven Quinn's car to Pinewood Close. He knew that Roope, or somebody working with him, had killed Quinn. And if it *wasn't* Roope, it had to be Bartlett.

'When I told Bartlett that Ogleby was in the Syndicate building that afternoon,' Morse continued, 'Bartlett understood that Ogleby knew the truth. So he or Roope murdered Ogleby too.'

'Why did you arrest Roope and then let him go?'

'I was hoping that Roope would lead us to Bartlett. And he did. He paid a newspaper boy to take a note to Bartlett. The note said that we knew about them and asked for help.'

Morse stopped.

'Is everything clear, Lewis?'

'Yes, sir – well – that is, no, not really. Bartlett spent many years working for the Syndicate. Why would he destroy its good reputation by selling exam papers?'

'People do strange things for money, Lewis,' Morse replied. 'Bartlett needed a lot of money for his son's treatment. Perhaps this was the only way that he could get it.'

———

That evening, Dr Bartlett was sitting alone in a small cold room at Police Headquarters. He had said nothing since his arrest. He was too shocked to speak.

The Syndicate building was empty except for Morse and Lewis. They were still sitting in Bartlett's office, looking through his desk and the drawers of his filing cabinets. In Bartlett's desk, Morse found a piece of the Syndicate's notepaper. There were five names at the top of the paper.

FOREIGN•EXAMINATIONS•SYNDICATE

T G Bartlett, Administrator
P Ogleby
~~*G Bland*~~
Mrs M Height
D J Martin

'The Syndicate will have to get some new notepaper now,' thought Morse. 'Three of these people no longer work here. One is dead, one is in Al-jamara, and the third is probably going to be in prison for the rest of his life!'

Morse read through the list of names again. Suddenly he shouted in surprise.

'Lewis!' he said. 'Take this piece of paper. Go and stand by the door. Read the first and last names on the list to me, but don't make any sound. Just use your lips.'

Lewis did what Morse asked him. 'Do it again!' Morse said.

Lewis read the names three more times – 'T.G. Bartlett' and 'D.J. Martin.'

'I've made a mistake, Lewis!' said Morse. 'A terrible mistake. Get your coat and come with me.'

———

Half an hour later, Morse and Lewis were at Donald Martin's house. Martin was not there, but his wife was at home.

Morse was talking to her angrily.

'Tell me the truth!' he said. 'Did your husband come home with blood on his coat last Friday evening? Answer me! Yes or no?'

Mrs Martin was frightened.

'Yes,' she said. 'I had to wash the blood off his coat. He said that he'd seen a car accident. He told me that he'd tried to help the driver.'

'There wasn't an accident,' said Morse. 'Your husband is a murderer. He killed Philip Ogleby that evening. It was Ogleby's blood on his coat.'

Mrs Martin began to cry. Suddenly the door opened and her husband rushed into the room. He began to attack Morse.

'What has that stupid man Roope told you?' he shouted.

Mrs Martin screamed and ran from the room. Martin went on hitting Morse. But Sergeant Lewis was stronger than Martin. He put his strong arms around the man and pulled him down onto the floor.

Later, when Martin had been taken to Police Headquarters and Bartlett had been driven home, Morse explained everything to Lewis.

'Quinn was a good lip-reader, but he made a serious mistake,' the inspector said. 'He read the *wrong* name on the lips of the Sheikh at that dinner.

'I learned at the lip-reading class that it's very easy to confuse the letters M and B in lip-reading. Quinn read "Doctor Bartlett" instead of "Donald Martin". The two names look the same on somebody's lips. So Quinn thought that *Bartlett* was working with Roope.

'Quinn was a very honest person. He told Roope that he knew the truth about the exam papers,' Morse continued. 'Roope told Martin that Quinn knew the truth. It was *Martin* who poisoned Quinn that morning. But Quinn had also told Ogleby about Bartlett. So Ogleby decided to search Bartlett's office for proof that Quinn was right. But he didn't find any proof because there was none to find. Bartlett hadn't done anything wrong.'

'I still don't understand about the cinema, sir,' Lewis said. 'Why did Mrs Height lie? And why did she ask Donald Martin to lie?'

'Monica didn't want me to find out that Bartlett was at the cinema because she wanted to protect his good reputation. She didn't want me to think that he went to see sexy films. That's why she lied about being at the cinema.'

'So Martin did everything that you said that Bartlett had done?' asked Lewis.

'Yes,' replied Morse. 'Martin killed Quinn. And Martin went back to the Syndicate building after the film had finished. He put the cinema ticket on Bartlett's desk because he knew that Roope would go into Bartlett's office and see it there. *Martin* wrote the note to Roope which told him to put the ticket in Quinn's pocket.'

'There's one more thing, sir,' said Lewis. 'Why did Roope ask the newspaper boy to take a note to Bartlett, and not to Martin?'

'Roope knew that we were watching him. He wanted to make us think that Bartlett was his partner. Then, when we found out that we were wrong about Bartlett, everyone would think that we were wrong about Roope too.'

'And why *did* Bartlett go to the Studio 2 cinema on Friday afternoon?'

Morse smiled.

'It's very simple, Lewis,' he said. 'Bartlett's life is difficult, because his son is very ill. Bartlett is often worried and unhappy. He want-  ed to forget his troubles for an hour. So he went to see a sexy Swedish film!'

All this happened several years ago. The Foreign Examinations Syndicate is closed now. It lost its good reputation when Roope and Martin were sent to prison for murder.

The Bartlett family moved away from Oxford. But Morse and Lewis had been wrong about them – the Bartletts were not poor people. Mrs Bartlett had a lot of money of her own. When the family left Oxford, she bought a farm. She lives peacefully there now with her husband and her son.

The Sheikh of Al-jamara's son, Muhammad Dubal, was disqualified from all his examinations – all his marks were cancelled. Six weeks later, there was a revolution in Al-jamara and the Sheikh disappeared. Al-jamara has a new ruler now – a good and honest man who is doing many great things for his country. George Bland left Al-jamara but he has never returned to the UK.

Monica Height is a school teacher now. She still goes to the Horse and Trumpet sometimes. She hopes to see Inspector Morse there. She liked him very much, and she would like to meet him again. But she never finds him.

Points for Understanding

1

What is the difference between the work of the Syndics and the work of the graduates who are permanent members of the Syndicate's staff?

2

After the dinner at the hotel, the Sheikh has conversations with several people. He thinks that these conversations are private, but they are not. Why not?

3

'Thank you for being honest,' the ticket collector says to Roope. Why does he say this?

4

1 What do Morse and Lewis find in Quinn's sitting-room?
2 'Please look in Quinn's fridge and make a list of what you find there,' Morse tells Lewis. Why do you think that Morse wants this information?

5

Why did Mrs Evans visit Number One, Pinewood Close twice on Friday, 21st November?

6

Constable Dickson tells Sally Height that he has seen a film about a dog on TV. Why?

7

When Morse talks to Roope, he thinks that the young man is like an actor in a play. Why does Morse think that Roope is behaving like this?

8

'Perhaps Quinn didn't return to Pinewood Close late on Friday. Perhaps he was murdered earlier that day,' Morse thinks. But later in the chapter, he thinks, 'My idea was wrong.' Why does he think that his idea was wrong?

9

Morse asks Lewis to find out when Richard Bartlett returned to the Littlemore Hospital, if he *did* return. Why does Morse want to know this?

10

Lewis visited Oxford railway station and talked to a taxi driver. Why did he do this?

11

Morse thinks that Roope changed the note which Quinn had left for his secretary.
(a) Why does Morse think that someone did this?
(b) What would be Roope's reason for changing the note?

12

Why does Morse think that Dr Bartlett was Roope's partner in the murder of Quinn?

13

Morse finds out that he has arrested the wrong person – he has arrested Dr Bartlett but he should have arrested Donald Martin. This has happened because Morse has made several mistakes. What are they?

Glossary

1 *set* (page 4)
questions are *set*, or prepared by *experts* (see Glossary Number 2, below). The questions are then put onto the exam papers.

2 *experts* (page 4)
people who know a lot about particular things.

3 *Administrator* (page 5)
the person in charge of the people who work in the Syndicate building.

4 *appoint* (page 5)
choose someone to do a job.

5 *interviewed* – *to interview* (page 6)
talk to someone who wants a job and ask them questions. The meeting at which this happens is called an *interview* (page 6). The person who wants the job and who is answering the questions is called an *interviewee* (page 6).

6 *crossly* (page 8)
the quick and sharp way someone speaks because they are angry.

7 *physical disability* (page 9)
be unable to move easily, or see easily, or hear easily.

8 *colleagues* (page 9)
when somebody works with other people, those people are his *colleagues*.

9 *room for improvement* (page 10)
it would be possible for things, or people, to work better.

10 *embarrassed* – *to be embarrassed* (page 10)
be uncomfortable because you have done something foolish.

11 **attractive** (page 11)
someone who has a beautiful or handsome face and body is *attractive*. A person is *attracted to someone* (page 25) if they think that that person is beautiful or handsome.

12 **pub** (page 11)
a public house, or a bar. Drinks and food can be bought in pubs. The bar is also the name given for the room in a pub where the drinks are sold at a long table. Most of the drinks which are sold in British pubs are alcoholic. The most popular drink in British pubs is beer.

13 **having an affair** – *to have an affair* (page 11)
have a romance or a sexual relationship with someone.

14 **first-class compartment** (page 16)
part of a railway train where passengers have larger, more comfortable seats. Food and drink is brought to the passengers by special railway staff. Passengers pay more money for tickets for first-class compartments.

15 **ticket barrier** (page 16)
gates at the entrance to a platform in a railway station. Passengers must show their tickets to railway officials at a *ticket barrier*.

16 **tip** (page 17)
extra money that you give to someone after you have paid them to do something. In Britain, tips are given to staff in hotels and restaurants, and taxi drivers, when they have done their work very well.

17 **filing cabinets** (page 18)
strong metal cupboards in which files and documents are kept.

18 **solved difficult cases** (page 19)
each new crime that the police have to find out about is called a *case*. Police work is called *investigation*. The police try to find out who commited the crime. Morse has to ask questions and think about each case. As soon as he knows what happened, when it happened and who committed the crime, he has *solved the case*.

19 **phone box** (page 20)
a tall box where you can make a phone call. There are phone boxes on streets, in railway stations, hotels etc.

20 **rent** – *to rent (to someone)* (page 21)
people pay Mrs Jardine money to live in the houses and apartments which she owns.

21 **sherry** (page 21)
a strong, sweet wine which is made in Spain and Portugal.

22 *cyanide* (page 21)
a poisonous liquid or a gas which has no colour. Cyanide has a smell like almonds. *Cyanide poisoning* (page 24) is extremely dangerous. You will die if you drink cyanide, or breathe cyanide gas.

23 *cleaner* (page 22)
a person who cleans the rooms in a house or an office.

24 *receipt* (page 22)
a piece of paper that you are given after you have paid for something. The receipt shows what you bought and how much money you paid.

25 *police doctor* (page 24)
a doctor who works for a police force. A *police doctor* looks after anyone who is hurt while they are in a police station. If the police find someone who has died or been murdered, police doctors also help them with their work.

26 *opinion* (page 24)
ideas about something or someone.

27 *go out with* – *to go out with someone* (page 26)
if you like someone very much and you spend a lot of time with them, you *go out with them*. You visit restaurants, museums, pubs, cinemas, etc.

28 *typed* (page 28)
a typewriter is a machine with a keyboard. You press the keys and words are *typed* immediately onto the paper. A few years ago, there were no computers in offices. Typewriters were used instead.

29 *official notepaper* (page 28)
notepaper which has the name and address of a company or institution printed at the top. Official notepaper sometimes also has the names of important people who work in the company.

30 *pathologist* (page 30)
a scientist who looks carefully at the bodies of dead people and the places where they were found. The *pathologist* then gives a report to the police.

31 *fingerprints* (page 30)
every person has marks on the ends of their fingers. When someone touches something, for example a piece of paper or a glass, shapes of these marks – *fingerprints* – are left on the things. Each person's fingerprints are different.

32 *fire drill* (page 31)
people who work together in buildings have *fire drills*. This is when they practise what to do if the building is on fire. Everyone leaves the building and stands in a safe place outside.

33 *security* (page 38)
the way that the exam papers are kept safe so that no one can read them or steal them before the students take the exams.

34 **wallet** (page 42)
a small leather case for carrying banknotes.

35 **local** (page 43)
local things are made for and by people living in a small area. A local newspaper is read by people who live in a town or city. National newspapers are read by everybody in the country.

36 **lose its good reputation** (page 44)
if everyone knows that a company behaves honestly, it has a *good reputation*. If a company starts to behave dishonestly, it *loses this good reputation*. A person can also have or lose a good reputation.

37 **mental illness** (page 56)
sickness of the mind.

38 *fainted* (page 58)
Monica saw Ogleby's dead body and she was very frightened and upset. A few minutes later, she fell onto the ground and was unable to see or hear for a short time. She had *fainted*.

39 **passenger door** (page 61)
a passenger may sit in a passenger seat which is in the front of a car, beside the driver. They can get in and out of the car through the *passenger door* which is next to them.

40 **inquest** (page 66)
when a person dies alone, or if they are killed by someone or something, a special meeting about the dead person takes place in a courtroom. This meeting is called an *inquest*. A doctor, police officers, and members of the dead person's family go to the court and tell a *coroner* (see below) what they know about that person.

41 **coroner** (page 67)
the official at an inquest who listens to reports from a doctor, police officers, and members of a dead person's family about the dead person. The *coroner* then decides if the person was murdered, or if their death was an accident.

42 **suspicions** (page 75)
because of the things that Roope has done, Morse thinks that he and someone else murdered Quinn. These thoughts are Morse's *suspicions*.

43 **boot** (page 78)
the place behind the seats in a car where you can put things. The *boot* of a car has a lid with a lock.

Published by Macmillan Heinemann ELT
Between Towns Road, Oxford OX4 3PP
Macmillan Heinemann ELT is an imprint of
Macmillan Publishers Limited
Companies and representatives throughout the world
Heinemann is a registered trademark of Harcourt Education, used under licence.

ISBN 1–405073–07–1
EAN 978–1–405073–07–3

The Silent World of Nicholas Quinn © Colin Dexter 1977
First published by Macmillan, an imprint of Macmillan Publishers Ltd,
25 Eccleston Place, London SW1W 9NF and Basingstoke

This retold version by Anne Collins for Macmillan Readers
First published 2000
Text © Macmillan Publishers Limited 2000, 2005
Design and illustration © Macmillan Publishers Limited 2000, 2005

This edition first published 2005

All rights reserved; no part of this publication may be reproduced,
stored in a retrieval system, transmitted in any form, or by any means,
electronic, mechanical, photocopying, recording, or otherwise, without
the prior written permission of the publishers.

Illustrated by Maureen Gray
Original cover template design by Jackie Hill
Cover photography by Alamy

Printed in Thailand

2009 2008 2007 2006 2005
10 9 8 7 6 5 4 3 2 1